The Old Nurse's Story/ Half a Li

by Elizabeth G

You know, my dears, that your mother was an orphan, and an only child; and I dare say you have heard that your grand-father was a clergyman up in Westmoreland, where I come from. I was just a girl in the village school, when, one day, your grandmother came in to ask the mistress if there was any scholar there who would do for a nurse-maid; and mighty proud I was, I can tell ye, when the mistress called me up, and spoke to my being a good girl at my needle, and a steady, honest girl, and one whose parents were very respectable, though they might be poor I thought I should like nothing better than to serve the pretty, young lady, who was blushing as deep as I was, as she spoke of the coming baby, and what I should have to do with it. However, I see you don't care so much for this part of my story, as for what you think is to come, so I'll tell you at once. I was engaged and settled at the parsonage before Miss Rosamond (that was the baby, who is now your mother) was born. To be sure, I had little enough to do with her when she came, for she was never out of her mother's arms, and slept by her all night long; and proud enough was I sometimes when missis trusted her to me. There never was such a baby before or since, though you've all of you been fine enough in your turns; but for sweet, winning ways, you've none of you come up to your mother. She took after her mother, who was a teal lady born; a Miss Furnivall, a granddaughter of Lord Furnivall's, in Northumberland. I believe she had neither brother nor Sister, and had been brought up in my lord's family till she had married your grandfather, who was just a curate, son to a shopkeeper in Carlisle - but a clever, fine gentleman as ever was - and one who was a right-down hard worker in his parish, which was very wide, and scattered all abroad over the Westmoreland Fells. When your mother, little Miss Rosamond, was about four or five years old, both her parents died in a fortnight - one after the other. Ah! that was a sad time. My pretty young mistress and me was looking for another baby, when my master came home from one of his long rides, wet, and tired, and took the fever he died of; and then she never held up her head again, but lived just to see her dead baby, and have it laid on her breast before she sighed away her life. My mistress had asked me, on her death-bed, never to leave Miss Rosamond; but if she had never spoken a word, I would have gone with the little child to the end of the world.

The next thing, and before we had well stilled our sobs, the executors and guardians came to settle the affairs. They were my poor young mistress's own cousin, Lord Furnivall, and Mr Esthwaite, my master's brother, a shopkeeper in Manchester; not so well to do then, as he was afterwards, and with a large family rising about him. Well! I don't know if it were their settling, or because of a letter my mistress wrote on her death-bed to her cousin, my lord; but somehow it was settled that Miss Rosamond and me were to go to Furnivall Manor House, in Northumberland, and my lord spoke as if it had been her mother's wish that she should live with his family, and as if he had no objectioins, for that one or two more or less could make no difference in so grand a household. So, though that was not the way in which I should have wished the coming of my bright and pretty pet to have been looked at - who was like a sunbeam in any family, be it never so grand - I was well pleased that all the folks in the Dale should stare and admire, when they heard I was going to be young lady's maid at my Lord Furnivall's at Furnivall Manor.

But I made a mistake in thinking we were to go and live where my lord did. It turned out that the family had left Furnivall Manor House fifty years or more. I could not hear that my poor young mistress had ever been there, though she had been brought up in the family; and I was sorry for that, for I should have liked Miss Rosamond's youth to have passed where her mother's had been.

My lord's gentleman, from whom I asked as many questions as I durst, said that the Manor House was at the foot of the Cumberland Fells, and a very grand place; that an old Miss Furnivall, a great-aunt of my lord's, lived there, with only a few servants; but that it was a very healthy place, and my lord had thought that it would suit Miss Rosamond very well for a few years, and that her being there might perhaps amuse his old aunt.

I was bidden by my lord to have Miss Rosamond's things ready by a certain day. He was a stern proud man, as they say all the Lords Furnivall were; and he never spoke a word more than was necessary. Folk did say he had loved my young mistress; but that, because she knew that his father would object, she would never listen to him, and married Esthwaite; but I don't know. He never married at any rate. But he never took much notice of Miss Rosamond; which I thought he might have done if he had cared for her dead mother. He sent his gentleman with us to the Manor House, telling him to join him at Newcastle that same evening; so there was no great length of time for him to make us known to all the strangers before he, too, shook us off; and we were left, two lonely young things (I was not eighteen), in the great old Manor House. It seems like yesterday that we drove there. We had left our own dear parsonage very early, and we had both cried as if our hearts would break, though we were travelling in my lord's carriage, which I thought so much of once. And now It was long past noon on a September day, and we stopped to change horses for the last time at a little, smoky town, all full of colliers and miners. Miss Rosamond had fallen asleep, but Mr Henry told me to waken her, that she might see the park and the Manor House as we drove up. I thought it rather a pity; but I did what he bade me, for fear he should complain of me to my lord. We had left all signs of a town, or even a village, and were then inside the gates of a large, wild park - not like the parks here in the south, but with rocks, and the noise of running water, and gnarled thorn-trees, and old oaks, all white and peeled with age.

The road went up about two miles, and then we saw a great and stately house, with many trees close around it, so close that in some places their branches dragged against the walls when the wind blew; and some hung broken down; for no one seemed to take much charge of the place; - to lop the wood, or to keep the moss-covered carriage-way in order. Only in front of the house all was clear. The great oval drive was without a weed; and neither tree nor creeper was allowed to grow over the long, many-windowed front; at both sides of which a wing projected, which were each the ends of other side fronts; for the house, although it was so desolate, was even grander than I expected. Behind it rose the Fells, which seemed unenclosed and bare enough; and on the left hand of the house, as you stood facing it, was a little, old-fashioned flower-garden, as I found out afterwards. A door opened out upon it from the west front; it had been scooped out of the thick dark wood for some old Lady Furnivall; but the branches of the great forest trees had grown and overshadowed it again, and there were very few flowers that would live there at that time. ▯@When we drove up to the great front entrance, and went into the hall I thought we should be lost - it was so large, and vast, and grand. There was a chandelier all of bronze, hung down from the middle of the ceiling; and I had never seen one before, and looked at it all in amaze. Then, at one end of the hall, was a great fireplace, as large as the sides of the houses in my country, with massy andirons and dogs to hold the wood; and by it were heavy, old-fashioned sofas. At the opposite end of the hall, to the left as you went in - on the western side - was an organ built into the wall, and so large that it filled up the best part of that end. Beyond it, on the same side, was a door; and opposite, on each side of the fire-place, were also doors leading to the east front; but those I never went through as long as I stayed in the house, so I can't tell you what lay beyond.

The afternoon was closing in and the hall, which had no fire lighted in it, looked dark and gloomy, but we did not stay there a moment. The old servant, who had opened the door for us bowed to Mr Henry, and took us in through the door at the further side of the great organ, and led us through several smaller halls and passages into the west drawing-room, where he said that Miss Furnivall was sitting. Poor little Miss Rosamond held very tight to me, as if she were scared and lost in that great place, and as for myself, I was not much better. The west drawing-room was very cheerful-looking, with a warm fire in it, and plenty of good, comfortable furniture about. Miss Furnivall was an old lady not far from eighty, I should think, but I do not know. She was thin and tall, and had a face as full of fine wrinkles as if they had been drawn all over it with a needle's point Her eyes were very watchful to make up, I suppose, for her being so deaf as to be obliged to use a trumpet. Sitting with her, working at the same great piece of tapestry, was Mrs Stark, her maid and companion, and almost as old as she was. She had lived with Miss Furnivall ever since they both were young, and now she seemed more like a friend than a servant; she looked so cold, and grey, and stony, as if she had never loved or cared for any one; and I don't suppose she did care for any one, except her mistress; and, owing to the great deafness of the latter,

Mrs Stark treated her very much as if she were a child. Mr Henry gave some message from my lord, and then he bowed good-bye to us all, - taking no notice of my sweet little Miss Rosamond's outstretched hand - and left us standing there, being looked at by the two old ladles through their spectacles.

I was right glad when they rung for the old footman who had shown us in at first, and told him to take us to our rooms. So we went out of that great drawing-room, and into another sitting-room, and out of that, and then up a great flight of stairs, and along a broad gallery - which was something like a library, having books all down one side, and windows and writing-tables all down the other - till we came to our rooms, which I was not sorry to hear were just over the kitchens; for I began to think I should be lost in that wilderness of a house. There was an old nursery, that had been used for all the little lords and ladies long ago, with a pleasant fire burning in the grate, and the kettle boiling on the bob, and tea things spread out on the table; and out of that room was the night-nursery, with a little crib for Miss Rosamond close to my bed. And old James called up Dorothy, his wife, to bid us welcome; and both he and she were so hospitable and kind, that by and by Miss Rosamond and me felt quite at home; and by the time tea was over, she was sitting on Dorothy's knee, and chattering away as fast as her little tongue could go. I soon found out that Dorothy was from Westmoreland, and that bound her and me together, as it were; and I would never wish to meet with kinder people than were old James and his wife. James had lived pretty nearly all his life in my lord's family, and thought there was no one so grand as they. He even looked down a little on his wife; because, till he had married her, she had never lived in any but a farmer's household. But he was very fond of her, as well he might be. They had one servant under them, to do all the rough work. Agnes they called her; and she and me, and James and Dorothy, with Miss Furnivall and Mrs Stark, made up the family; always remembering my sweet little Miss Rosamond! I used to wonder what they had done before she came, they thought so much of her now. Kitchen and drawing-room, it was all the same. The hard, sad Miss Furnivall, and the cold Mrs Stark, looked pleased when she came fluttering in like a bird, playing and pranking hither and thither, with a continual murmur, and pretty prattle of gladness. I am sure, they were sorry many a time when she flitted away into the kitchen, though they were too proud to ask her to stay with them, and were a little surprised at her taste; though to be sure, as Mrs Stark said, it was not to be wondered at, remembering what stock her father had come of. The great, old rambling house was a famous place for little Miss Rosamond. She made expeditions all over it, with me at her heels; all, except the east wing, which was never opened, and whither we never thought of going. But in the western and northern part was many a pleasant room; full of things that were curiosities to us, though they might not have been to people who had seen more. The windows were darkened by the sweeping boughs of the trees, and the ivy which had overgrown them: but, in the green gloom, we could manage to see old China jars and carved ivory boxes, and great, heavy books, and, above all, the old pictures!

Once, I remember, my darling would have Dorothy go with us to tell us who they all were; for they were all portraits of some of my lord's family, though Dorothy could not tell us the names of every one. We had gone through most of the rooms, when we came to the old state drawing-room over the hall, and there was a picture of Miss Furnivall; or, as she was called in those days, Miss Grace, for she was the younger sister. Such a beauty she must have been! but with such a set, proud look, and such scorn looking out of her handsome eyes, with her eyebrows just a little raised, as if she wondered how any one could have the impertinence to look at her; and her lip curled at us, as we stood there gazing. She had a dress on, the like of which I had never seen before, but it was all the fashion when she was young: a hat of some soft, white stuff like beaver, pulled a little over her brows, and a beautiful plume of feathers sweeping round it on one side; and her gown of blue satin was open in front to a quilted, white stomacher.

'Well, to be sure!' said I, when I had gazed my fill. 'Flesh is grass, they do say; but who would have thought that Miss Furnivall had been such an out-and-out beauty, to see her now?'

'Yes,' said Dorothy. 'Folks change sadly. But if what my master's father used to say was true, Miss Furnivall, the elder sister, was handsomer thin Miss Grace. Her picture is here somewhere; but, if I show it you, you must never let on, even to James, that you have seen it. Can the little lady hold her tongue, think you?' asked she.

I was not so sure, for she was such a little, sweet, bold, open-spoken child, so I set her to hide herself; and then I helped Dorothy to turn a great picture, that leaned with its face towards the wall, and was not hung up as the others were. To be sure, it beat Miss Grace for beauty; and, I think, for scornful pride, too, though in that matter it might be hard to choose. I could have looked at it an hour, but Dorothy seemed half frightened at having shown it to me, and hurried it back again, and bade me run and find Miss Rosamond, for that there were some ugly places about the house, where she should like ill for the child to go. I was a brave, high-spirited girl, and thought little of what the old woman said, for I liked hide-and-seek as well as any child in the parish; so off I ran to find my little one.

As winter drew on, and the days grew shorter, I was sometimes almost certain that I heard a noise as if some one was playing on the great organ in the hall. I did not hear it every evening; but, certainly, I did very often; usually when I was sitting with Miss Rosamond, after I had put her to bed, and keeping quite still and silent in the bed-room. Then I used to hear it booming and swelling away in the distance. The first night, when I went down to my supper, I asked Dorothy who had been playing music, and James said very shortly that I was a gowk to take the wind soughing among the trees for music: but I saw Dorothy look at him very fearfully, and Agnes, the kitchen-maid, said something beneath her breath, and went quite white. I saw they did not like my question, so I held my peace till I was with Dorothy alone, when I knew I could get a good deal out of her. So, the next day, I watched my time, and I coaxed and asked her who it was that played the organ; for I knew that it was the organ and not the wind well enough, for all I had kept silence before James. But Dorothy had had her lesson I'll warrant, and never a word could I get from her. So then I tried Agnes, though I had always held my head rather above her, as I was even to James and Dorothy, and she was little better than their servant. So she said I must never, never tell; and if I ever told, I was never to say she had told me; but it was a very strange noise, and she had heard it many a time, but most of all on winter nights, and before storms; and folks did say, it was the old lord playing on the great organ in the hall, just as he used to do when he was alive; but who the old lord was, or why he played, and why he played on stormy winter evenings in particular, she either could not or would not tell me. Well! I told you I had a brave heart; and I thought it was rather pleasant to have that grand music rolling about the house, let who would be the player; for now it rose above the great gusts of wind, and wailed and triumphed just like a living creature, and then it fell to a softness most complete; only it was always music, and tunes, so it was nonsense to call it the wind I thought at first, that it might be Miss Furnivall who played, unknown to Agnes; but, one day when I was in the hall by myself, I opened the organ and peeped all about it and around it, as I had done to the organ in Crosthwaite Ghurch once before, and I saw it was all broken and destroyed inside, though it looked so brave and fine; and then, though it was noon-day, my flesh began to creep a little, and I shut it up, and run away pretty quickly to my own bright nursery; and I did not like hearing the music for some time after that, any more than James and Dorothy did. All this time Miss Rosamond was making herself more and more beloved. The old ladies liked her to dine with them at their early dinner; James stood behind Miss Furnivall's chair, and I behind Miss Rosamond's all in state; and, after dinner, she would play about in a corner of the great drawing-room, as still as any mouse, while Miss Furnivall slept, and I had my dinner in the kitchen. But she was glad enough to come to me in the nursery afterwards; for, as she said, Miss Furnivall was so sad, and Mrs Stark so dull; but she and I were merry enough; and, by-and-by, I got not to care for that weird rolling music, which did one no harm, if we did not know where it came from. ⁊@That winter was very cold. In the middle of October the frosts began, and lasted many, many weeks. I remember, one day at dinner, Miss Furnivall lifted up her sad, heavy eyes, and said to Mrs Stark, 'I am afraid we shall have a terrible winter,' in a strange kind of meaning way. But Mrs Stark pretended not to hear, and talked very loud of something else. My little lady and I did not care for the frost; not we! As long as it was dry we climbed up the steep brows, behind the house, and went up on the Fells, which were bleak, and bare enough, and there we ran races in the fresh, sharp air; and once we came down by a new path that took us past the two old, gnarled holly-trees, which grew about half-way down by the east side of the house. But the days grew shorter, and shorter; and the old lord, if it was he, played away more, and more stormily and sadly on the great organ. One Sunday afternoon, - it must have been towards the end of November - I asked Dorothy to take charge of little Missey when she came out of the drawing-room, after Miss Furnivall had had her nap; for it was too cold to take her with me to church, and yet I wanted to go. And Dorothy was glad enough to promise, and was so fond of the child that all seemed well; and Agnes and I set off very briskly, though the sky hung heavy and black over the white earth, as if the night had never fully gone away; and the air, though still, was very biting and keen.

'We shall have a fall of snow,' said Agnes to me. And sure enough, even while we were in church, it came down thick, in great, large flakes, so thick it almost darkened the windows. It had stopped snowing before we came out, but it lay soft, thick and deep beneath our feet, as we tramped home. Before we got to the hall the moon rose, and I think it was lighter then, - what with the moon, and what with the white dazzling snow - than it had been when we went to church, between two and three o'clock. I have not told you that Miss Furnivall and Mrs Stark never went to church: they used to read the prayers together, in their quiet, gloomy way; they seemed to feel the Sunday very long without their tapestry-work to be busy at. So when I went to Dorothy in the kitchen, to fetch Miss Rosamond and take her up-stairs with me, I did not much wonder when the old woman told me that the ladies had kept the child with them, and that she had never come to the kitchen, as I had bidden her, when she was tired of behaving pretty in the drawing-room. So I took off my things and went to find her, and bring her to her supper in the nursery. But when I went into the best drawing-room, there sate the two old ladies, very still and quiet, dropping out a word now and then, but looking as if nothing so bright and merry as Miss Rosamond had ever been near them. Still I thought she might be hiding from me; it was one of her pretty ways; and that she had persuaded them to look as if they knew nothing about her; so I went softly peeping under this sofa, and behind that chair, making believe I was sadly frightened at not finding her.

'What's the matter, Hester?' said Mrs Stark sharply. I don't know if Miss Furnivall had seen me, for, as I told you, she was very deaf, and she sate quite still, idly staring into the fire, with her hopeless face. 'I'm only looking for my little Rosy-Posy,' replied I, still thinking that the child was there, and near me, though I could not see her.

'Miss Rosamond is not here,' said Mrs Stark. 'She went away more than an hour ago to find Dorothy.' And she too turned and went on looking into the fire.

My heart sank at this, and I began to wish I had never left my darling. I went back to Dorothy and told her. James was gone out for the day, but she and me and Agnes took lights and went up into the nursery first, and then we roamed over the great large house, calling and entreating Miss Rosamond to come out of her hiding place, and not frighten us to death in that way. But there was no answer; no sound.

'Oh!' said I at last. 'Can she have got into the east wing and hidden there?'

But Dorothy said it was not possible, for that she herself had never been in there; that the doors were always locked, and my lord's steward had the keys, she believed; at any rate, neither she nor James had ever seen them: so, I said I would go back, and see if, after all, she was not hidden in the drawing-room, unknown to the old ladies; and if I found her there, I said, I would whip her well for the fright she had given me; but I never meant to do it. Well, I went hack to the west drawing-room, and I told Mrs Stark we could not find her anywhere, and asked for leave to look all about the furniture there, for I thought now, that she might have fallen asleep in some warm, hidden comer; but no! we looked, Miss Furnivall got up and looked, trembling all over, and she was no where there; then we set off again, every one in the house, and looked in all the places we had searched before, but we could not find her.

Miss Furnivall shivered and shook so much, that Mrs Stark took her back into the warm drawing-room; but not before they had made me promise to bring her to them when she was found. Well-a-day! I began to think she never would be found, when I bethought me to look out into the great front court, all covered with snow. I was up-stairs when I looked out; but, it was such dear moonlight, I could see quite plain two little footprints, which might be traced from the hall door, and round the comer of the east wing. I don't know how I got down, but I tugged open the great,stiff hall door; and, throwing the skirt of my gown over head for a cloak, I ran out. I turned the east comer, and there a black shadow fell on the snow; but when I came again into the moonlight, there were the little footmarks going up - up to the Fells. It was bitter cold; so cold that the air almost took the skin off my face as I ran, but I ran on, crying to think how my poor little darling must be perished, and frightened. I was within sight of the holly-trees, when I saw a shepherd coming down the hill, bearing something in his arms wrapped in his maud. He shouted to me, and asked me if I had lost a bairn; and, when I could not speak for crying, he bore towards me, and I saw my wee bairnie lying still, and white, and stiff, in his arms, as if she had been dead. He told me he had been up the Fells to gather in his sheep, before the deep cold of night came on, and that under the holly-trees (black marks on the hill-side, where no other bush was for miles around) he had found my little lady - my lamb - my queen - my darling - stiff, and cold, in the terrible sleep which is frost-begotten. Oh! the joy, and the tears, of having her in my arms once again! for I would not let him carry her; but took her, maud and all, into my own arms, and held her near my own warm neck, and heart, and felt the life stealing slowly back again into her little, gentle limbs. But she was still insensible when we reached the hall, and I had no breath for speech. We went in by the kitchen door.

'Bring the warming-pan,' said I; and I carried her up-stairs and began undressing her by the nursery fire, which Agnes had kept up. I called my little lammie all the sweet and playful names I could think of, - even while my eyes were blinded by my tears; and at last, oh! at length she opened her large, blue eyes. Then I put her into her warm bed, and sent Dorothy down to tell

Miss Furnivall that all was well; and I made up my mind to sit by my darling's bedside the live-long night. She fell away into a soft sleep as soon as her pretty head had touched the pillow, and I watched by her till morning light; when she wakened up bright and clear - or so I thought at first - and, my dears, so I think now.

She said, that she had fancied that she should like to go to Dorothy, for that both the old ladies were asleep, and it was very dull in the drawing-room; and that, as she was going through the west lobby, she saw the snow through the high window failing - falling - soft and steady; but she wanted to see it lying pretty and white on the ground; so she made her way into the great hall; and then, going to the window, she saw it bright and soft upon the drive; but while she stood there, she saw a little girl, not as old as she was, 'but so pretty,' said my darling, 'and this little girl beckoned to me to come out; and oh, she was so pretty and so sweet, I could not choose but go.' And then this other little girl had taken her by the hand, and side by side the two had gone round the east corner.

'Now, you are a naughty little girl, and telling stories,' said I. 'What would your good mamma, that is in heaven, and never told a story in her life, say to her little Rosamond, if she heard her - and I dare say she does - telling stories!'

'Indeed, Hester,' sobbed out my child, 'I'm telling you true. Indeed I am.'

'Don't tell me!' said I, very stern. 'I tracked you by your foot-marks through the snow; there were only yours to be seen: and if you had had a little girl to go hand-in-hand with you up the hill, don't you think the foot-prints would have gone along with yours?'

'I can't help it, dear, dear Hester,' said she, crying, 'if they did not; I never looked at her feet, but she held my hand fast and tight in her little one, and it was very, very cold. She took me up the Fell-path, up to the holly trees; and there I saw a lady weeping and crying; but when she saw me, she hushed her weeping, and smiled very proud and grand, and took me on her knee, and began to lull me to sleep; and that's all, Hester - but that is true; and my dear mamma knows it is,' said she, crying. So I thought the child was in a fever, and pretended to believe her, as she went over her story - over and over again, and always the same. At last Dorothy knocked at the door with Miss Rosamond's breakfast; and she told me the old ladies were down in the eating parlour, and that they wanted to speak to me. They had both been into the night-nursery the evening before, but it was after Miss Rosamond was asleep; so they had only looked at her - not asked me any questions.

'I shall catch it,' thought I to myself, as I went along the north gallery. 'And yet,' I thought, taking courage, 'it was in their charge I left her; and it's they that's to blame for letting her steal away unknown and unwatched.' So I went in boldly, and told my story. I told it all to Miss Furnivall, shouting it close to her ear; but when I came to the mention of the other little girl out in the snow, coaxing and tempting her out, and her up to the grand and beautiful lady by the holly-tree, she threw her arms up - her old and withered arms - and cried aloud, 'Oh! Heaven, forgive! Have mercy!'

Mrs Stark took hold of her; roughly enough, I thought; but she was past Mrs Stark's management, and spoke to me, in a kind of wild warning and authority.

'Hester! keep her from that child! It will lure her to her death! That evil child! Tell her it is a wicked, naughty child' Then, Mrs Stark hurried me out of the room; where, indeed, I was glad enough to go; but Miss Furnivall kept shrieking out, 'Oh! have mercy! Wilt Thou never forgive! It is many a long year ago - '

I was very uneasy in my mind after that. I durst never leave Miss Rosamond, night or day, for fear lest she might slip off again, after some fancy or other; and all the more, because I thought I could make out that Miss Furnivall was crazy, from their odd ways about her; and I was afraid lest something of the same kind (which might be in the family, you know) hung over my darling.

And the great frost never ceased all this time; and, whenever it was a more stormy night than usual, between the gusts, and through the wind, we heard the old lord playing on the great organ. But, old lord, or not, wherever Miss Rosamond went, there I followed; for my love for her, pretty, helpless orphan, was stronger than my fear for the grand and terrible sound. Besides, it rested with me to keep her cheerful and merry, as beseemed her age. So we played together, and wandered together, here and there, and every- where; for I never dared to lose sight of her again in that large and rambling house. And so it happened, that one afternoon, not long before Christmas day, we were playing together on the billiard-table in the great hall (not that we knew the right way of playing, but she liked to roll the smooth ivory balls with her pretty hands, and I liked to do whatever she did); and, by-and-by, without our noticing it, it grew dusk indoors, though it was still light in the open air, and I was thinking of taking her back into the nursery, when, all of sudden, she cried out, -

'Look, Hester! look! there is my poor little girl out in the snow!'

I turned towards the long, narrow windows, and there, sure Snow!' enough, I saw a little girl, less than my Miss Rosamond dressed all unfit to be out-of-doors such a bitter night - crying, and beating against the window-panes, as if she wanted to be let in. She seemed to sob and wail, till Miss Rosamond could bear it no longer, and was flying to the door to open it, when, all of a sudden, and close upon us, the great organ pealed out so loud and thundering, it fairly made me tremble; and all the more, when I remembered me that, even in the stillness of that dead-cold weather, I had heard no sound of little battering hands upon the window-glass, although the Phantom Child had seemed to put forth all its force; and, although I had seen it wail and cry, no faintest touch of sound had fallen upon my ears. whether I remembered all this at the very moment, I do not know; the great organ sound had so stunned me into terror; but this I know, I caught up Miss Rosamond before she got the hall-door opened, and clutched her, and carried her away, kicking and screaming, into the large, bright kitchen, where Dorothy and Agnes were busy with their mince-pies.

What is the matter with my sweet one?' cried Dorothy, as I bore in Miss Rosamond, who was sobbing as if her heart would break.

'She won't let me open the door for my little girl to come in; and she'll die if she is out on the Fells all night. Cruel, naughty Hester,' she said, slapping me; but she might have struck harder, for I had seen a look of ghastly terror on Dorothy's face, which made my very blood run cold.

'Shut the back kitchen door fast, and bolt it well,' said she to Agnes. She said no more; she gave me raisins and almonds to quiet Miss Rosamond: but she sobbed about the little girl in the snow, and would not touch any of the good things. I was thankful when she cried herself to sleep in bed. Then I stole down to the kitchen, and told Dorothy I had made up my mind I would carry my darling back to my father's house in Applethwaite; where, if we lived humbly, we lived at peace. I said I had been frightened enough with the old lord's organ-playing; but now that I had seen for myself this little, moaning child, all decked out as no child in the neighbourhood could be, beating and battering to get in, yet always without any sound or noise - with the dark wound on its right shoulder; and that Miss Rosamond had known it again for the phantom that had nearly lured her to her death (which Dorothy knew was true); I would stand it no longer.

I saw Dorothy change colour once or twice. When I had done, she told me she did not think I could take Miss Rosamond with me, for that she was my lord's ward, and I had no right over her; and she asked me, would I leave the child that I was so fond of, just for sounds and sights that could do me no harm; and that they had all had to get used to in their turns? I was all in a hot, trembling passion; and I said it was very well for her to talk, that knew what these sights and noises betokened, and that had, perhaps, had something to do with the Spectre-Child while it was alive. And I taunted her so, that she told me all she knew, at last; and then I wished I had never been told, for it only made me more afraid than ever.

She said she had heard the tale from old neighbours, that were alive when she was first married; when folks used to come to the hall sometimes, before it had got such a bad name on the country side: it might not be true, or it might, what she had been told.

The old lord was Miss Furnivall's father - Miss Grace, as Dorothy called her, for Miss Maude was the elder, and Miss Furnivall by rights. The old lord was eaten up with pride. Such a proud man was never seen or heard of; and his daughters were like him. No one was good enough to wed them, although they had choice enough; for they were the great beauties of their day, as I had seen by their portraits, where they hung in the state drawing-room. But, as the old saying is, 'Pride will have a fall'; and these two haughty beauties fell in love with the same man, and he no better than a foreign musician, whom their father had down from London to play music with him at the Manor House. For, above all things,next to his pride, the old lord loved music. He could play on nearly every instrument that ever was heard of: and it was a strange thing it did not soften him; but he was a fierce, dour, old man, and had broken his poor wife's heart with his cruelty, they said. He was mad after music, and would pay any money for it. So he got this foreigner to come; who made such beautiful music, that they said the very birds on the trees stopped their singing to listen. And, by degrees, this foreign gentleman got such a hold over the old lord, that nothing would serve him but that he must come every year; and it was he that had the great organ brought from Holland, and built up in the hall, ' where it stood now. He taught the old lord to play on it; hut many and many a time, when Lord Furnivall was thinking of nothing but his fine organ, and his finer music, the dark foreigner was walking abroad in the woods with one of the young ladies; now Miss Maude, and then Miss Grace.

Miss Maude won the day and carried off the prize, such as it was; and he and she were married, all unknown to any one; and before he made his next yearly visit, she had been confined of a little girl at a farm-house on the Moors, while her father and Miss Grace thought she was away at Doncaster Races. But though she was a wife and a mother, she was not a bit softened, but as haughty and as passionate as ever; and perhaps more so' for she was jealous of Miss Grace, to whom her foreign husband paid a deal of court - by way of blinding her - as he told his wife. But Miss Grace triumphed over Miss Maude, and Miss Maude grew fiercer and fiercer, both with her husband and with her sister; and the former who could easily shake off what was disagreeable, and hide himself in foreign countries - went away a month before his usual time that summer, and half-threatened that he would never come back again. Meanwhile, the little girl was left at the farm-house, and her mother used to have her horse saddled and gallop wildly over the hills to see her once every week, at the very least - for where she loved, she loved; and where she hated, she hated. And the old lord went on playing - playing on his organ; and the servants thought the sweet music he made had soothed down his awful temper, of which (Dorothy said) some terrible tales could be told. He grew infirm too, and had to walk with a crutch; and his son - that was the present Lord Furnivall's father - was with the army in America, and the other son at sea; so Miss Maude had it pretty much her own way, and she and Miss Grace grew colder and bitterer to each other every day; till at last they hardly ever spoke, except when the old lord was by. The foreign musician came again the next summer, but it was for the last time; for they led him such a life with their jealousy and their passions, that he grew weary, and went away, and never was heard of again. And Miss Maude, who had always meant to have her marriage acknowledged when her father should be dead, was left now a deserted wife - whom nobody knew to have been married - with a child that she dared not own, although she loved it to distraction; living with a father whom she feared, and a sister whom she hated. When the next summer passed over and the dark foreigner never came, both Miss Maude and Miss Grace grew gloomy and sad; they had a haggard look about them, though they looked handsome as ever. But by-and-by Miss Maude brightened; for her father grew more and more infirm, and more than ever carried away by his music; and she and Miss Grace lived almost entirely apart, having separate rooms, the one on the west side, Miss Maude on the east - those very rooms which were now shut up. So she thought she might have her little girl with her, and no one need ever know except those who dared not speak about it, and were bound to believe that it was, as she said, a cottager's child she had taken a fancy to. All this Dorothy said, was pretty well known; but what came afterwards no one knew, except Miss Grace, and Mrs Stark, who was even then her maid, and much more of a friend to her than ever her sister had been. But the servants supposed, from words that were dropped, that Miss Maude had triumphed over Miss Grace, and told her that all the time the dark foreigner had been mocking her with pretended love - he was her own husband; the colour left Miss Grace's cheek and lips that very day for ever, and she was heard to say many a time that sooner or later she would have her revenge; and Mrs Stark was for ever spying about the east rooms.

One fearful night, just after the New Year had come in, when the snow was lying thick and deep, and the flakes were still falling - fast enough to blind any one who might be out and abroad - there was a great and violent noise heard, and the old lord's voice above all, cursing and swearing awfully, - and the cries of a little child, - and the proud defiance of a fierce woman, - and the sound of a blow, - and a dead stillness, - and moans and wailing's dying away on the hill-side! Then the old lord summoned all his servants, and told them, with terrible oaths, and words more terrible, that his daughter had disgraced herself, and that he had turned her out of doors, - her, and her child, - and that if ever they gave her help, - or food, - or shelter, - he prayed that they might never enter Heaven. And, all the while, Miss Grace stood by him, white and still as any stone; and when he had ended she heaved a great sigh, as much as to say her work was done, and her end was accomplished. But the old lord never touched his organ again, and died within the year; and no wonder! for, on the morrow of that wild and fearful night, the shepherds, coming down the Fell-side, found Miss Maude sitting, all crazy and smiling, under the holly-trees,nursing a dead child, - with a terrible mark on its right shoulder. 'But that was not what killed it,' said; 'it was the frost and the cold; - every wild creature was in its hole, and every beast in its fold, - while the child and its mother were turned out to wander on the Fells! And now you know all! and I wonder if you are less frightened now?'

I was more frightened than ever; but I said I was not. I wished Miss Rosamond and myself well out of that dreadful house for ever; but I would not leave her, and I dared not take her away. But oh! how I watched her, and guarded her! We bolted the doors, and shut the window-shutters fast, an hour or more before dark, rather than leave them open five minutes too late. But my little lady still heard the weird child crying and mourning; and not all we could do or say, could keep her from wanting to go to her, and let her in from the cruel wind and the snow. All this time, I kept away from Miss Furnivall and Mrs Stark, as much as ever I could; for I feared them - I knew no good could be about them, with their grey hard faces, and their dreamy eyes, looking back into the ghastly years that were gone. But, even in my fear, I had a kind of pity - for Miss Furnivall, at least. Those gone down to the pit can hardly have a more hopeless look than that which was ever on her face. At last I even got so sorry for her - who never said a word but what was quite forced from her - that I prayed for her; and I taught Miss Rosamond to pray for one who had done a deadly sin; but often when she came to those words, she would listen, and start up from her knees, and say, 'I hear my little girl plaining and crying very sad - Oh! let her in, or she will die!'

One night - just after New Year's Day had come at last, and the long winter had taken a turn, as I hoped - I heard the west drawing-room bell ring three times, which was the signal for me. I would not leave MissRosamond alone, for all she was asleep - for the old lord had been playing wilder than ever - and I feared lest my darling should waken to hear the spectre child; see her I knew she could not. I had fastened the windows too well for that. So, I took her out of her bed and wrapped her up in such outer clothes as were most handy, and carried her down to the drawing-room, where the old ladies sate at their tapestry work as usual. They looked up when I came in, and Mrs Stark asked, quite astounded, 'Why did I bring Miss Rosamond there, out of her warm bed?' I had begun to whisper, 'Because I was afraid of her being tempted out while I was away, by the wild child in the snow,' when she stopped me short (with a glance at Miss Furnivall), and said Miss Furnivall wanted me to undo some work she had done wrong, and which neither of them could see to unpick. So, I laid my pretty dear on the sofa, and sate down on a stool by them, and hardened my heart against them, as I heard the wind rising and howling.

Miss Rosamond slept on sound, for all the wind blew so; and Miss Furnivall said never a word, nor looked round when the gusts shook the windows. All at once she started up to her full height, and put up one hand, as if to bid us listen.

'I hear voices!' said she. 'I hear terrible screams - I hear my father's voice!'

Just at that moment, my darling wakened with a sudden start: 'My little girl is crying, oh, how she is crying!' and she tried to get up and go to her, but she got her feet entangled in the blanket, and I caught her up; for my flesh had begun to creep at these noises, which they heard while we could catch no sound. In a minute or two the noises came, and gathered fast, and filled our ears; we, too, heard voices and screams, and no longer heard the winter's wind that raged abroad. Mrs Stark looked at me, and I at her, but we dared not speak.Suddenly Miss Furnivall went towards the door, out into the ante-room, through the west lobby, and opened the door into the great hall. Mrs Stark followed, and I durst not be left, though my heart almost stopped beating for fear. I wrapped my darling tight in my arms, and went out with them. In the hall the screams were louder than ever; they sounded to come from the east wing - nearer and nearer - close on the other side of the locked-up doors - close behind them. Then I noticed that the great bronze chandelier seemed all alight, though the hall was dim, and that a fire was blazing in the vast hearth-place, though it gave no heat; and I shuddered up with terror, and folded my darling closer to me. But as I did so, the east door shook, and she, suddenly struggling to get free from me, cried, 'Hester! I must go! My little girl is there; I hear her; she is coming! Hester, I must go!'

I held her tight with all my strength; with a set will, I held her. If I had died, my hands would have grasped her still, I was so resolved in my mind. Miss Furnivall stood listening, and paid no regard to my darling, who had got down to the ground, and whom I, upon my knees now, was holding with both my arms clasped round her neck; she still striving and crying to get free. @@

All at once, the east door gave way with a thundering crash, as if torn open in a violent passion, and there came into that broad and mysterious light, the figure of a tall, old man, with grey hair and gleaming eyes. He drove before him, with many a relentless gesture of abhorrence, a stern and beautiful woman, with a little child clinging to her dress.

'Oh Hester! Hester!' cried Miss Rosamond. 'It's the lady! the lady below the holly-trees; and my little girl is with her. Hester! Hester! let me go to her; they are drawing me to them. I feel them - I feel them. I must go!'

Again she was almost convulsed by her efforts to get away; but I held her tighter and tighter, till I feared I should do her a hurt; but rather that than let her go towards those terrible phantoms. They passed along towards the great hall-door, where the winds howled and ravened for their prey; but before they reached that, the lady turned; and I could see that she defied the old man with a fierce and proud defiance; but then she quailed - and then she threw her arms wildly and piteously to save her child - her little child - from a blow from his uplifted crutch.

And Miss Rosamond was torn as by a power stronger thin mine, and writhed in my arms, and sobbed (for by this time the poor darling was growing faint).

'They want me to go with them on to the Fells - they are drawing me to them. Oh, my little girl! I would come, but cruel, wicked Hester holds me very tight.' But when she saw the uplifted crutch she swooned away, and I thanked God for it. Just at this moment - when the tall, old man, his hair streaming as in the blast of a furnace, was going to strike the little, shrinking child - Miss Furnivall, the old woman by my side, cried out, 'Oh, father! father! spare the little, innocent child!' But just then I saw - we all saw - another phantom shape itself, and grow clear out of the blue and misty light that filled the hall; we had not seen her till now, for it was another lady who stood by the old man, with a look of relentless hate and triumphant scorn. That figure was very beautiful to look upon, with a soft, white hat drawn down over the proud brows, and a red and curling lip. It was dressed in an open robe of blue satin. I had seen that figure before. It was the likeness of Miss Furnivall in her youth; and the terrible phantoms moved on, regardless of old Miss Furnivall's wild entreaty, and the uplifted crutch fell on the right shoulder of the little child, and the younger sister looked on, stony and deadly serene. But at that moment, the dim lights, and the fire that gave no heat, went out of themselves, and Miss Furnivall lay at our feet stricken down by the palsy - death-stricken.

Yes! she was carried to her bed that night never to rise again. She lay with her face to the wall, muttering low, but muttering always: Alas! alas! what is done in youth can never be undone in age! what is done in youth can never be undone in age!'

Half a Life-time Ago

by Elizabeth Gaskel

Chapter I

Half a life-time ago, there lived in one of the Westmoreland dales a single woman, of the name of Susan Dixon. She was owner of the small farm-house where she resided, and of some thirty or forty acres of land by which it was surrounded. She had also an hereditary right to a sheep-walk, extending to the wild fells that overhang Blea Tarn. In the language of the country she was a Stateswoman. Her house is yet to be seen on the Oxenfell road, between Skelwith and Coniston. You go along a moorland track, made by the carts that occasionally came for turf from the Oxenfell. A brook babbles and brattles by the wayside, giving you a sense of companionship, which relieves the deep solitude in which this way is usually traversed. Some miles on this side of Coniston there is a farmstead--a gray stone house, and a square of farm-buildings surrounding a green space of rough turf, in the midst of which stands a mighty, funereal umbrageous yew, making a solemn shadow, as of death, in the very heart and centre of the light and heat of the brightest summer day. On the side away from the house, this yard slopes down to a dark-brown pool, which is supplied with fresh water from the overflowings of a stone cistern, into which some rivulet of the brook before-mentioned continually and melodiously falls bubbling. The cattle drink out of this cistern. The household bring their pitchers and fill them with drinking-water by a dilatory, yet pretty, process. The water-carrier brings with her a leaf of the hound's-tongue fern, and, inserting it in the crevice of the gray rock, makes a cool, green spout for the sparkling stream.

The house is no specimen, at the present day, of what it was in the lifetime of Susan Dixon. Then, every small diamond pane in the windows glittered with cleanliness. You might have eaten off the floor; you could see yourself in the pewter plates and the polished oaken awmry, or dresser, of the state kitchen into which you entered. Few strangers penetrated further than this room. Once or twice, wandering tourists, attracted by the lonely picturesqueness of the situation, and the exquisite cleanliness of the house itself, made their way into this house-place, and offered money enough (as they thought) to tempt the hostess to receive them as lodgers. They would give no trouble, they said; they would be out rambling or sketching all day long; would be perfectly content with a share of the food which she provided for herself; or would procure what they required from the Waterhead Inn at Coniston. But no liberal sum--no fair words--moved her from her stony manner, or her monotonous tone of indifferent refusal. No persuasion could induce her to show any more of the house than that first room; no appearance of fatigue procured for the weary an invitation to sit down and rest; and if one more bold and less delicate did so without being asked, Susan stood by, cold and apparently deaf, or only replying by the briefest monosyllables, till the unwelcome visitor had departed. Yet those with whom she had dealings, in the way of selling her cattle or her farm produce, spoke of her as keen after a bargain--a hard one to have to do with; and she never spared herself exertion or fatigue, at market or in the field, to make the most of her produce. She led the hay-makers with her swift, steady rake, and her noiseless evenness of motion. She was about among the earliest in the market, examining samples of oats, pricing them, and then turning with grim satisfaction to her own cleaner corn.

She was served faithfully and long by those who were rather her fellow-labourers than her servants. She was even and just in her dealings with them. If she was peculiar and silent, they knew her, and knew that she might be relied on. Some of them had known her from her childhood; and deep in their hearts was an unspoken--almost unconscious--pity for her, for they knew her story, though they never spoke of it.

Yes; the time had been when that tall, gaunt, hard-featured, angular woman--who never smiled, and hardly ever spoke an unnecessary word--had been a fine-looking girl, bright-spirited and rosy; and when the hearth at the Yew Nook had been as bright as she, with family love and youthful hope and mirth. Fifty or fifty-one years ago, William Dixon and his wife Margaret were alive; and Susan, their daughter, was about eighteen years old--ten years older than the only other child, a boy named after his father. William and Margaret Dixon were rather superior people, of a character belonging--as far as I have seen--exclusively to the class of Westmoreland and Cumberland statesmen--just, independent, upright; not given to much speaking; kind-hearted, but not demonstrative; disliking change, and new ways, and new people; sensible and shrewd; each household self-contained, and its members having little curiosity as to their neighbours, with whom they rarely met for any social intercourse, save at the stated times of sheep-shearing and Christmas; having a certain kind of sober pleasure in amassing money, which occasionally made them miserable (as they call miserly people up in the north) in their old age; reading no light or ephemeral literature, but the grave, solid books brought round by the pedlars (such as the "Paradise Lost" and "Regained,'" "The Death of Abel," "The Spiritual Quixote," and "The Pilgrim's Progress"), were to be found in nearly every house: the men occasionally going off laking, i.e. playing, i.e. drinking for days together, and having to be hunted up by anxious wives, who dared not leave their husbands to the chances of the wild precipitous roads, but walked miles and miles, lantern in hand, in the dead of night, to discover and guide the solemnly-drunken husband home; who had a dreadful headache the next day, and the day after that came forth as grave, and sober, and virtuous looking as if there were no such thing as malt and spirituous liquors in the world; and who were seldom reminded of their misdoings by their wives, to whom such occasional outbreaks were as things of course, when once the immediate anxiety produced by them was over. Such were--such are--the characteristics of a class now passing away from the face of the land, as their compeers, the yeomen, have done before them. Of such was William Dixon. He was a shrewd clever farmer, in his day and generation, when shrewdness was rather shown in the breeding and rearing of sheep and cattle than in the cultivation of land. Owing to this character of his, statesmen from a distance from beyond Kendal, or from Borrowdale, of greater wealth than he, would send their sons to be farm-servants for a year or two with him, in order to learn some of his methods before setting up on land of their own. When Susan, his daughter, was about seventeen, one Michael Hurst was farm-servant at Yew Nook. He worked with the master, and lived with the family, and was in all respects treated as an equal, except in the field. His father was a wealthy statesman at Wythburne, up beyond Grasmere; and through Michael's servitude the families had become acquainted, and the Dixons went over to the High Beck sheep-shearing, and the Hursts came down by Red Bank and Loughrig Tarn and across the Oxenfell when there was the Christmas-tide feasting at Yew Nook. The fathers strolled round the fields together, examined cattle and sheep, and looked knowing over each other's horses. The mothers inspected the dairies and household arrangements, each openly admiring the plans of the other, but secretly preferring their own. Both fathers and mothers cast a glance from time to time at Michael and Susan, who were thinking of nothing less than farm or dairy, but whose unspoken attachment was, in all ways, so suitable and natural a thing that each parent rejoiced over it, although with characteristic reserve it was never spoken about--not even between husband and wife.

Susan had been a strong, independent, healthy girl; a clever help to her mother, and a spirited companion to her father; more of a man in her (as he often said) than her delicate little brother ever would have. He was his mother's darling, although she loved Susan well. There was no positive engagement between Michael and Susan--I doubt whether even plain words of love had been spoken; when one winter- time Margaret Dixon was seized with inflammation consequent upon a neglected cold. She had always been strong and notable, and had been too busy to attend to the early symptoms of illness. It would go off, she said to the woman who helped in the kitchen; or if she did not feel better when they had got the hams and bacon out of hand, she would take some herb-tea and nurse up a bit. But Death could not wait till the hams and bacon were cured: he came on with rapid strides, and shooting arrows of portentous agony. Susan had never seen illness--never knew how much she loved her mother till now, when she felt a dreadful, instinctive certainty that she was losing her. Her mind was thronged with recollections of the many times she had slighted her mother's wishes; her heart was full of the echoes of careless and angry replies that she had spoken. What would she not now give to have opportunities of service and obedience, and trials of her patience and love, for that dear mother who lay gasping in torture! And yet Susan had been a good girl and an affectionate daughter.

The sharp pain went off, and delicious ease came on; yet still her mother sunk. In the midst of this languid peace she was dying. She motioned Susan to her bedside, for she could only whisper; and then, while the father was out of the room, she spoke as much to the eager, hungering eyes of her daughter by the motion of her lips, as by the slow, feeble sounds of her voice.

"Susan, lass, thou must not fret. It is God's will, and thou wilt have a deal to do. Keep father straight if thou canst; and if he goes out Ulverstone ways, see that thou meet him before he gets to the Old Quarry. It's a dree bit for a man who has had a drop. As for lile Will"--Here the poor woman's face began to work and her fingers to move nervously as they lay on the bed-quilt--"lile Will will miss me most of all. Father's often vexed with him because he's not a quick strong lad; he is not, my poor lile chap. And father thinks he's saucy, because he cannot always stomach oat-cake and porridge. There's better than three pound in th' old black tea-pot on the top shelf of the cupboard. Just keep a piece of loaf-bread by you, Susan dear, for Will to come to when he's not taken his breakfast. I have, may be, spoilt him; but there'll be no one to spoil him now."

She began to cry a low, feeble cry, and covered up her face that Susan might not see her. That dear face! those precious moments while yet the eyes could look out with love and intelligence. Susan laid her head down close by her mother's ear.

"Mother I'll take tent of Will. Mother, do you hear? He shall not want ought I can give or get for him, least of all the kind words which you had ever ready for us both. Bless you! bless you! my own mother."

"Thou'lt promise me that, Susan, wilt thou? I can die easy if thou'lt take charge of him. But he's hardly like other folk; he tries father at times, though I think father'll be tender of him when I'm gone, for my sake. And, Susan, there's one thing more. I never spoke on it for fear of the bairn being called a tell-tale, but I just comforted him up. He vexes Michael at times, and Michael has struck him before now. I did not want to make a stir; but he's not strong, and a word from thee, Susan, will go a long way with Michael."

Susan was as red now as she had been pale before; it was the first time that her influence over Michael had been openly acknowledged by a third person, and a flash of joy came athwart the solemn sadness of the moment. Her mother had spoken too much, and now came on the miserable faintness. She never spoke again coherently; but when her children and her husband stood by her bedside, she took lile Will's hand and put it into Susan's, and looked at her with imploring eyes. Susan clasped her arms round Will, and leaned her head upon his little curly one, and vowed within herself to be as a mother to him.

Henceforward she was all in all to her brother. She was a more spirited and amusing companion to him than his mother had been, from her greater activity, and perhaps, also, from her originality of character, which often prompted her to perform her habitual actions in some new and racy manner. She was tender to lile Will when she was prompt and sharp with everybody else--with Michael most of all; for somehow the girl felt that, unprotected by her mother, she must keep up her own dignity, and not allow her lover to see how strong a hold he had upon her heart. He called her hard and cruel, and left her so; and she smiled softly to herself, when his back was turned, to think how little he guessed how deeply he was loved. For Susan was merely comely and fine looking; Michael was strikingly handsome, admired by all the girls for miles round, and quite enough of a country coxcomb to know it and plume himself accordingly. He was the second son of his father; the eldest would have High Beck farm, of course, but there was a good penny in the Kendal bank in store for Michael. When harvest was over, he went to Chapel Langdale to learn to dance; and at night, in his merry moods, he would do his steps on the flag floor of the Yew Nook kitchen, to the secret admiration of Susan, who had never learned dancing, but who flouted him perpetually, even while she admired, in accordance with the rule she seemed to have made for herself about keeping him at a distance so long as he lived under the same roof with her. One evening he sulked at some saucy remark of hers; he sitting in the chimney corner with his arms on his knees, and his head bent forwards, lazily gazing into the wood-fire on the hearth, and luxuriating in rest after a hard day's labour; she sitting among the geraniums on the long, low window-seat, trying to catch the last slanting rays of the autumnal light to enable her to finish stitching a shirt-collar for Will, who lounged full length on the flags at the other side of the hearth to Michael, poking the burning wood from time to time with a long hazel-stick to bring out the leap of glittering sparks.

"And if you can dance a threesome reel, what good does it do ye?" asked Susan, looking askance at Michael, who had just been vaunting his proficiency. "Does it help you plough, reap, or even climb the rocks to take a raven's nest? If I were a man, I'd be ashamed to give in to such softness."

"If you were a man, you'd be glad to do anything which made the pretty girls stand round and admire."

"As they do to you, eh! Ho, Michael, that would not be my way o' being a man!"

"What would then?" asked he, after a pause, during which he had expected in vain that she would go on with her sentence. No answer.

"I should not like you as a man, Susy; you'd be too hard and headstrong."

"Am I hard and headstrong?" asked she, with as indifferent a tone as she could assume, but which yet had a touch of pique in it. His quick ear detected the inflexion.

"No, Susy! You're wilful at times, and that's right enough. I don't like a girl without spirit. There's a mighty pretty girl comes to the dancing class; but she is all milk and water. Her eyes never flash like yours when you're put out; why, I can see them flame across the kitchen like a cat's in the dark. Now, if you were a man, I should feel queer before those looks of yours; as it is, I rather like them, because--"

"Because what?" asked she, looking up and perceiving that he had stolen close up to her.

"Because I can make all right in this way," said he, kissing her suddenly.

"Can you?" said she, wrenching herself out of his grasp and panting, half with rage. "Take that, by way of proof that making right is none so easy." And she boxed his ears pretty sharply. He went back to his seat discomfited and out of temper. She could no longer see to look, even if her face had not burnt and her eyes dazzled, but she did not choose to move her seat, so she still preserved her stooping attitude and pretended to go on sewing.

"Eleanor Hebthwaite may be milk-and-water," muttered he, "but--Confound thee, lad! what art thou doing?" exclaimed Michael, as a great piece of burning wood was cast into his face by an unlucky poke of Will's. "Thou great lounging, clumsy chap, I'll teach thee better!" and with one or two good round kicks he sent the lad whimpering away into the back-kitchen. When he had a little recovered himself from his passion, he saw Susan standing before him, her face looking strange and almost ghastly by the reversed position of the shadows, arising from the firelight shining upwards right under it.

"I tell thee what, Michael," said she, "that lad's motherless, but not friendless."

"His own father leathers him, and why should not I, when he's given me such a burn on my face?" said Michael, putting up his hand to his cheek as if in pain.

"His father's his father, and there is nought more to be said. But if he did burn thee, it was by accident, and not o' purpose; as thou kicked him, it's a mercy if his ribs are not broken."

"He howls loud enough, I'm sure. I might ha' kicked many a lad twice as hard, and they'd ne'er ha' said ought but 'damn ye;' but yon lad must needs cry out like a stuck pig if one touches him;" replied Michael, sullenly.

Susan went back to the window-seat, and looked absently out of the window at the drifting clouds for a minute or two, while her eyes filled with tears. Then she got up and made for the outer door which led into the back-kitchen. Before she reached it, however, she heard a low voice, whose music made her thrill, say -

"Susan, Susan!"

Her heart melted within her, but it seemed like treachery to her poor boy, like faithlessness to her dead mother, to turn to her lover while the tears which he had caused to flow were yet unwiped on Will's cheeks. So she seemed to take no heed, but passed into the darkness, and, guided by the sobs, she found her way to where Willie sat crouched among the disused tubs and churns.

"Come out wi' me, lad;" and they went out into the orchard, where the fruittrees were bare of leaves, but ghastly in their tattered covering of gray moss: and the soughing November wind came with long sweeps over the fells till it rattled among the crackling boughs, underneath which the brother and sister sat in the dark; he in her lap, and she hushing his head against her shoulder.

"Thou should'st na' play wi' fire. It's a naughty trick. Thoul't suffer for it in worse ways nor this before thou'st done, I'm afeared. I should ha' hit thee twice as lungeous kicks as Mike, if I'd been in his place. He did na' hurt thee, I am sure," she assumed, half as a question.

"Yes but he did. He turned me quite sick." And he let his head fall languidly down on his sister's breast.

"Come, lad! come, lad!" said she anxiously. "Be a man. It was not much that I saw. Why, when first the red cow came she kicked me far harder for offering to milk her before her legs were tied. See thee! here's a peppermint-drop, and I'll make thee a pasty to-night; only don't give way so, for it hurts me sore to think that Michael has done thee any harm, my pretty."

Willie roused himself up, and put back the wet and ruffled hair from his heated face; and he and Susan rose up, and hand-in-hand went towards the house, walking slowly and quietly except for a kind of sob which Willie could not repress. Susan took him to the pump and washed his tear-stained face, till she thought she had obliterated all traces of the recent disturbance, arranging his curls for him, and then she kissed him tenderly, and led him in, hoping to find Michael in the kitchen, and make all straight between them. But the blaze had dropped down into darkness; the wood was a heap of gray ashes in which the sparks ran hither and thither; but even in the groping darkness Susan knew by the sinking at her heart that Michael was not there. She threw another brand on the hearth and lighted the candle, and sat down to her work in silence. Willie cowered on his stool by the side of the fire, eyeing his sister from time to time, and sorry and oppressed, he knew not why, by the sight of her grave, almost stern face. No one came. They two were in the house alone. The old woman who helped Susan with the household work had gone out for the night to some friend's dwelling. William Dixon, the father, was up on the fells seeing after his sheep. Susan had no heart to prepare the evening meal.

"Susy, darling, are you angry with me?" said Willie, in his little piping, gentle voice. He had stolen up to his sister's side. "I won't never play with the fire again; and I'll not cry if Michael does kick me. Only don't look so like dead mother--don't--don't--please don't!" he exclaimed, hiding his face on her shoulder.

"I'm not angry, Willie," said she. "Don't be feared on me. You want your supper, and you shall have it; and don't you be feared on Michael. He shall give reason for every hair of your head that he touches--he shall."

When William Dixon came home he found Susan and Willie sitting together, hand-in-hand, and apparently pretty cheerful. He bade them go to bed, for that he would sit up for Michael; and the next morning, when Susan came down, she found that Michael had started an hour before with the cart for lime. It was a long day's work; Susan knew it would be late, perhaps later than on the preceding night, before he returned--at any rate, past her usual bed-time; and on no account would she stop up a minute beyond that hour in the kitchen, whatever she might do in her bed-room. Here she sat and watched till past midnight; and when she saw him coming up the brow with the carts, she knew full well, even in that faint moonlight, that his gait was the gait of a man in liquor. But though she was annoyed and mortified to find in what way he had chosen to forget her, the fact did not disgust or shock her as it would have done many a girl, even at that day, who had not been brought up as Susan had, among a class who considered it no crime, but rather a mark of spirit, in a man to get drunk occasionally. Nevertheless, she chose to hold herself very high all the next day when Michael was, perforce, obliged to give up any attempt to do heavy work, and hung about the out-buildings and farm in a very disconsolate and sickly state. Willie had far more pity on him than Susan. Before evening, Willie and he were fast, and, on his side, ostentatious friends. Willie rode the horses down to water; Willie helped him to chop wood. Susan sat gloomily at her work, hearing an indistinct but cheerful conversation going on in the shippon, while the cows were being milked. She almost felt irritated with her little brother, as if he were a traitor, and had gone over to the enemy in the very battle that she was fighting in his cause. She was alone with no one to speak to, while they prattled on regardless if she were glad or sorry.

Soon Willie burst in. "Susan! Susan! come with me; I've something so pretty to show you. Round the corner of the barn--run! run!" (He was dragging her along, half reluctant, half desirous of some change in that weary day. Round the corner of the barn; and caught hold of by Michael, who stood there awaiting her.

"O Willie!" cried she "you naughty boy. There is nothing pretty--what have you brought me here for? Let me go; I won't be held."

"Only one word. Nay, if you wish it so much, you may go," said Michael, suddenly loosing his hold as she struggled. But now she was free, she only drew off a step or two, murmuring something about Willie.

"You are going, then?" said Michael, with seeming sadness. "You won't hear me say a word of what is in my heart."

"How can I tell whether it is what I should like to hear?" replied she, still drawing back.

"That is just what I want you to tell me; I want you to hear it and then to tell me whether you like it or not."

"Well, you may speak," replied she, turning her back, and beginning to plait the hem of her apron.

He came close to her ear.

"I'm sorry I hurt Willie the other night. He has forgiven me. Can you?"

"You hurt him very badly," she replied. "But you are right to be sorry. I forgive you."

"Stop, stop!" said he, laying his hand upon her arm. "There is something more I've got to say. I want you to be my--what is it they call it, Susan?"

"I don't know," said she, half-laughing, but trying to get away with all her might now; and she was a strong girl, but she could not manage it.

"You do. My--what is it I want you to be?"

"I tell you I don't know, and you had best be quiet, and just let me go in, or I shall think you're as bad now as you were last night."

"And how did you know what I was last night? It was past twelve when I came home. Were you watching? Ah, Susan! be my wife, and you shall never have to watch for a drunken husband. If I were your husband, I would come straight home, and count every minute an hour till I saw your bonny face. Now you know what I want you to be. I ask you to be my wife. Will you, my own dear Susan?"

She did not speak for some time. Then she only said "Ask father." And now she was really off like a lapwing round the corner of the barn, and up in her own little room, crying with all her might, before the triumphant smile had left Michael's face where he stood.

The "Ask father" was a mere form to be gone though. Old Daniel Hurst and William Dixon had talked over what they could respectively give their children before this; and that was the parental way of arranging such matters. When the probable amount of worldly gear that he could give his child had been named by each father, the young folk, as they said, might take their own time in coming to the point which the old men, with the prescience of experience, saw they were drifting to; no need to hurry them, for they were both young, and Michael, though active enough, was too thoughtless, old Daniel said, to be trusted with the entire management of a farm. Meanwhile, his father would look about him, and see after all the farms that were to be let.

Michael had a shrewd notion of this preliminary understanding between the fathers, and so felt less daunted than he might otherwise have done at making the application for Susan's hand. It was all right, there was not an obstacle; only a deal of good advice, which the lover thought might have as well been spared, and which it must be confessed he did not much attend to, although he assented to every part of it. Then Susan was called down stairs, and slowly came dropping into view down the steps which led from the two family apartments into the house-place. She tried to look composed and quiet, but it could not be done. She stood side by side with her lover, with her head drooping, her cheeks burning, not daring to look up or move, while her father made the newly-betrothed a somewhat formal address in which he gave his consent, and many a piece of worldly wisdom beside. Susan listened as well as she could for the beating of her heart; but when her father solemnly and sadly referred to his own lost wife, she could keep from sobbing no longer; but throwing her apron over her face, she sat down on the bench by the dresser, and fairly gave way to pent-up tears. Oh, how strangely sweet to be comforted as she was comforted, by tender caress, and many a low-whispered promise of love! Her father sat by the fire, thinking of the days that were gone; Willie was still out of doors; but Susan and Michael felt no one's presence or absence--they only knew they were together as betrothed husband and wife.

In a week, or two, they were formally told of the arrangements to be made in their favour. A small farm in the neighbourhood happened to fall vacant; and Michael's father offered to take it for him, and be responsible for the rent for the first year, while William Dixon was to contribute a certain amount of stock, and both fathers were to help towards the furnishing of the house. Susan received all this information in a quiet, indifferent way; she did not care much for any of these preparations, which were to hurry her through the happy hours; she cared least of all for the money amount of dowry and of substance. It jarred on her to be made the confidante of occasional slight repinings of Michael's, as one by one his future father-in-law set aside a beast or a pig for Susan's portion, which were not always the best animals of their kind upon the farm. But he also complained of his own father's stinginess, which somewhat, though not much, alleviated Susan's dislike to being awakened out of her pure dream of love to the consideration of worldly wealth.

But in the midst of all this bustle, Willie moped and pined. He had the same chord of delicacy running through his mind that made his body feeble and weak. He kept out of the way, and was apparently occupied in whittling and carving uncouth heads on hazel-sticks in an out-house. But he positively avoided Michael, and shrunk away even from Susan. She was too much occupied to notice this at first. Michael pointed it out to her, saying, with a laugh, -

"Look at Willie! he might be a cast-off lover and jealous of me, he looks so dark and downcast at me." Michael spoke this jest out loud, and Willie burst into tears, and ran out of the house.

"Let me go. Let me go!" said Susan (for her lover's arm was round her waist). "I must go to him if he's fretting. I promised mother I would!" She pulled herself away, and went in search of the boy. She sought in byre and barn, through the orchard, where indeed in this leafless winter-time there was no great concealment; up into the room where the wool was usually stored in the later summer, and at last she found him, sitting at bay, like some hunted creature, up behind the wood-stack.

"What are ye gone for, lad, and me seeking you everywhere?" asked she, breathless.

"I did not know you would seek me. I've been away many a time, and no one has cared to seek me," said he, crying afresh.

"Nonsense," replied Susan, "don't be so foolish, ye little good-for-nought." But she crept up to him in the hole he had made underneath the great, brown sheafs of wood, and squeezed herself down by him. "What for should folk seek after you, when you get away from them whenever you can?" asked she.

"They don't want me to stay. Nobody wants me. If I go with father, he says I hinder more than I help. You used to like to have me with you. But now, you've taken up with Michael, and you'd rather I was away; and I can just bide away; but I cannot stand Michael jeering at me. He's got you to love him and that might serve him."

"But I love you, too, dearly, lad!" said she, putting her arm round his neck.

"Which on us do you like best?" said he, wistfully, after a little pause, putting her arm away, so that he might look in her face, and see if she spoke truth.

She went very red.

"You should not ask such questions. They are not fit for you to ask, nor for me to answer."

"But mother bade you love me!" said he, plaintively.

"And so I do. And so I ever will do. Lover nor husband shall come betwixt thee and me, lad--ne'er a one of them. That I promise thee (as I promised mother before), in the sight of God and with her hearkening now, if ever she can hearken to earthly word again. Only I cannot abide to have thee fretting, just because my heart is large enough for two."

"And thou'lt love me always?"

"Always, and ever. And the more--the more thou'lt love Michael," said she, dropping her voice.

"I'll try," said the boy, sighing, for he remembered many a harsh word and blow of which his sister knew nothing. She would have risen up to go away, but he held her tight, for here and now she was all his own, and he did not know when such a time might come again. So the two sat crouched up and silent, till they heard the horn blowing at the field-gate, which was the summons home to any wanderers belonging to the farm, and at this hour of the evening, signified that supper was ready. Then the two went in.

Chapter II

Susan and Michael were to be married in April. He had already gone to take possession of his new farm, three or four miles away from Yew Nook--but that is neighbouring, according to the acceptation of the word in that thinly-populated district,--when William Dixon fell ill. He came home one evening, complaining of head-ache and pains in his limbs, but seemed to loathe the posset which Susan prepared for him; the treacle-posset which was the homely country remedy against an incipient cold. He took to his bed with a sensation of exceeding weariness, and an odd, unusual looking-back to the days of his youth, when he was a lad living with his parents, in this very house.

The next morning he had forgotten all his life since then, and did not know his own children; crying, like a newly-weaned baby, for his mother to come and soothe away his terrible pain. The doctor from Coniston said it was the typhus-fever, and warned Susan of its infectious character, and shook his head over his patient. There were no near friends to come and share her anxiety; only good, kind old Peggy, who was faithfulness itself, and one or two labourers' wives, who would fain have helped her, had not their hands been tied by their responsibility to their own families. But, somehow, Susan neither feared nor flagged. As for fear, indeed, she had no time to give way to it, for every energy of both body and mind was required. Besides, the young have had too little experience of the danger of infection to dread it much. She did indeed wish, from time to time, that Michael had been at home to have taken Willie over to his father's at High Beck; but then, again, the lad was docile and useful to her, and his fecklessness in many things might make him harshly treated by strangers; so, perhaps, it was as well that Michael was away at Appleby fair, or even beyond that--gone into Yorkshire after horses.

Her father grew worse; and the doctor insisted on sending over a nurse from Coniston. Not a professed nurse--Coniston could not have supported such a one; but a widow who was ready to go where the doctor sent her for the sake of the payment. When she came, Susan suddenly gave way; she was felled by the fever herself, and lay unconscious for long weeks. Her consciousness returned to her one spring afternoon; early spring: April,--her wedding-month. There was a little fire burning in the small corner-grate, and the flickering of the blaze was enough for her to notice in her weak state. She felt that there was some one sitting on the window-side of her bed, behind the curtain, but she did not care to know who it was; it was even too great a trouble for her languid mind to consider who it was likely to be. She would rather shut her eyes, and melt off again into the gentle luxury of sleep. The next time she wakened, the Coniston nurse perceived her movement, and made her a cup of tea, which she drank with eager relish; but still they did not speak, and once more Susan lay motionless--not asleep, but strangely, pleasantly conscious of all the small chamber and household sounds; the fall of a cinder on the hearth, the fitful singing of the half-empty kettle, the cattle tramping out to field again after they had been milked, the aged step on the creaking stair--old Peggy's, as she knew. It came to her door; it stopped; the person outside listened for a moment, and then lifted the wooden latch, and looked in. The watcher by the bedside arose, and went to her. Susan would have been glad to see Peggy's face once more, but was far too weak to turn, so she lay and listened.

"How is she?" whispered one trembling, aged voice.

"Better," replied the other. "She's been awake, and had a cup of tea. She'll do now."

"Has she asked after him?"

"Hush! No; she has not spoken a word."

"Poor lass! poor lass!"

The door was shut. A weak feeling of sorrow and self-pity came over Susan. What was wrong? Whom had she loved? And dawning, dawning, slowly rose the sun of her former life, and all particulars were made distinct to her. She felt that some sorrow was coming to her, and cried over it before she knew what it was, or had strength enough to ask. In the dead of night,--and she had never slept again,--she softly called to the watcher, and asked -

"Who?"

"Who what?" replied the woman, with a conscious affright, ill-veiled by a poor assumption of ease. "Lie still, there's a darling, and go to sleep. Sleep's better for you than all the doctor's stuff."

"Who?" repeated Susan. "Something is wrong. Who?"

"Oh, dear!" said the woman. "There's nothing wrong. Willie has taken the turn, and is doing nicely."

"Father?"

"Well! he's all right now," she answered, looking another way, as if seeking for something.

"Then it's Michael! Oh, me! oh, me!" She set up a succession of weak, plaintive, hysterical cries before the nurse could pacify her, by declaring that Michael had been at the house not three hours before to ask after her, and looked as well and as hearty as ever man did.

"And you heard of no harm to him since?" inquired Susan.

"Bless the lass, no, for sure! I've ne'er heard his name named since I saw him go out of the yard as stout a man as ever trod shoe- leather."

It was well, as the nurse said afterwards to Peggy, that Susan had been so easily pacified by the equivocating answer in respect to her father. If she had pressed the questions home in his case as she did in Michael's, she would have learnt that he was dead and buried more than a month before. It was well, too, that in her weak state of convalescence (which lasted long after this first day of consciousness) her perceptions were not sharp enough to observe the sad change that had taken place in Willie. His bodily strength returned, his appetite was something enormous, but his eyes wandered continually; his regard could not be arrested; his speech became slow, impeded, and incoherent. People began to say that the fever had taken away the little wit Willie Dixon had ever possessed and that they feared that he would end in being a "natural," as they call an idiot in the Dales.

The habitual affection and obedience to Susan lasted longer than any other feeling that the boy had had previous to his illness; and, perhaps, this made her be the last to perceive what every one else had long anticipated. She felt the awakening rude when it did come. It was in this wise:-

One Jane evening, she sat out of doors under the yew-tree, knitting. She was pale still from her recent illness; and her languor, joined to the fact of her black dress, made her look more than usually interesting. She was no longer the buoyant self-sufficient Susan, equal to every occasion. The men were bringing in the cows to be milked, and Michael was about in the yard giving orders and directions with somewhat the air of a master, for the farm belonged of right to Willie, and Susan had succeeded to the guardianship of her brother. Michael and she were to be married as soon as she was strong enough--so, perhaps, his authoritative manner was justified; but the labourers did not like it, although they said little. They remembered a stripling on the farm, knowing far less than they did, and often glad to shelter his ignorance of all agricultural matters behind their superior knowledge. They would have taken orders from Susan with far more willingness; nay, Willie himself might have commanded them; and from the old hereditary feeling toward the owners of land, they would have obeyed him with far greater cordiality than they now showed to Michael. But Susan was tired with even three rounds of knitting, and seemed not to notice, or to care, how things went on around her; and Willie--poor Willie!--there he stood lounging against the door-sill, enormously grown and developed, to be sure, but with restless eyes and ever-open mouth, and every now and then setting up a strange kind of howling cry, and then smiling vacantly to himself at the sound he had made. As the two old labourers passed him, they looked at each other ominously, and shook their heads.

"Willie, darling," said Susan, "don't make that noise--it makes my head ache."

She spoke feebly, and Willie did not seem to hear; at any rate, he continued his howl from time to time.

"Hold thy noise, wilt'a?" said Michael, roughly, as he passed near him, and threatening him with his fist. Susan's back was turned to the pair. The expression of Willie's face changed from vacancy to fear, and he came shambling up to Susan, who put her arm round him, and, as if protected by that shelter, he began making faces at Michael. Susan saw what was going on, and, as if now first struck by the strangeness of her brother's manner, she looked anxiously at Michael for an explanation. Michael was irritated at Willie's defiance of him, and did not mince the matter.

"It's just that the fever has left him silly--he never was as wise as other folk, and now I doubt if he will ever get right."

Susan did not speak, but she went very pale, and her lip quivered. She looked long and wistfully at Willie's face, as he watched the motion of the ducks in the great stable-pool. He laughed softly to himself every now and then.

"Willie likes to see the ducks go overhead," said Susan, instinctively adopting the form of speech she would have used to a young child.

"Willie, boo! Willie, boo!" he replied, clapping his hands, and avoiding her eye.

"Speak properly, Willie," said Susan, making a strong effort at self-control, and trying to arrest his attention.

"You know who I am--tell me my name!" She grasped his arm almost painfully tight to make him attend. Now he looked at her, and, for an instant, a gleam of recognition quivered over his face; but the exertion was evidently painful, and he began to cry at the vainness of the effort to recall her name. He hid his face upon her shoulder with the old affectionate trick of manner. She put him gently away, and went into the house into her own little bedroom. She locked the door, and did not reply at all to Michael's calls for her, hardly spoke to old Peggy, who tried to tempt her out to receive some homely sympathy, and through the open easement there still came the idiotic sound of "Willie, boo! Willie, boo!"

Chapter III

After the stun of the blow came the realization of the consequences. Susan would sit for hours trying patiently to recall and piece together fragments of recollection and consciousness in her brother's mind. She would let him go and pursue some senseless bit of play, and wait until she could catch his eye or his attention again, when she would resume her self-imposed task. Michael complained that she never had a word for him, or a minute of time to spend with him now; but she only said she must try, while there was yet a chance, to bring back her brother's lost wits. As for marriage in this state of uncertainty, she had no heart to think of it. Then Michael stormed, and absented himself for two or three days; but it was of no use. When he came back, he saw that she had been crying till her eyes were all swollen up, and he gathered from Peggy's scoldings (which she did not spare him) that Susan had eaten nothing since he went away. But she was as inflexible as ever.

"Not just yet. Only not just yet. And don't say again that I do not love you," said she, suddenly hiding herself in his arms.

And so matters went on through August. The crop of oats was gathered in; the wheat-field was not ready as yet, when one fine day Michael drove up in a borrowed shandry, and offered to take Willie a ride. His manner, when Susan asked him where he was going to, was rather confused; but the answer was straight and clear enough.

He had business in Ambleside. He would never lose sight of the lad, and have him back safe and sound before dark. So Susan let him go.

Before night they were at home again: Willie in high delight at a little rattling paper windmill that Michael had bought for him in the street, and striving to imitate this new sound with perpetual buzzings. Michael, too, looked pleased. Susan knew the look, although afterwards she remembered that he had tried to veil it from her, and had assumed a grave appearance of sorrow whenever he caught her eye. He put up his horse; for, although he had three miles further to go, the moon was up--the bonny harvest-moon--and he did not care how late he had to drive on such a road by such a light. After the supper which Susan had prepared for the travellers was over, Peggy went up-stairs to see Willie safe in bed; for he had to have the same care taken of him that a little child of four years old requires.

Michael drew near to Susan.

"Susan," said he, "I took Will to see Dr. Preston, at Kendal. He's the first doctor in the county. I thought it were better for us--for you--to know at once what chance there were for him."

"Well!" said Susan, looking eagerly up. She saw the same strange glance of satisfaction, the same instant change to apparent regret and pain. "What did he say?" said she. "Speak! can't you?"

"He said he would never get better of his weakness."

"Never!"

"No; never. It's a long word, and hard to bear. And there's worse to come, dearest. The doctor thinks he will get badder from year to year. And he said, if he was us--you--he would send him off in time to Lancaster Asylum. They've ways there both of keeping such people in order and making them happy. I only tell you what he said," continued he, seeing the gathering storm in her face.

"There was no harm in his saying it," she replied, with great self-constraint, forcing herself to speak coldly instead of angrily. "Folk is welcome to their opinions."

They sat silent for a minute or two, her breast heaving with suppressed feeling.

"He's counted a very clever man," said Michael at length.

"He may be. He's none of my clever men, nor am I going to be guided by him, whatever he may think. And I don't thank them that went and took my poor lad to have such harsh notions formed about him. If I'd been there, I could have called out the sense that is in him."

"Well! I'll not say more to-night, Susan. You're not taking it rightly, and I'd best be gone, and leave you to think it over. I'll not deny they are hard words to hear, but there's sense in them, as I take it; and I reckon you'll have to come to 'em. Anyhow, it's a bad way of thanking me for my pains, and I don't take it well in you, Susan," said he, getting up, as if offended.

"Michael, I'm beside myself with sorrow. Don't blame me if I speak sharp. He and me is the only ones, you see. And mother did so charge me to have a care of him! And this is what he's come to, poor lile chap!" She began to cry, and Michael to comfort her with caresses.

"Don't," said she. "It's no use trying to make me forget poor Willie is a natural. I could hate myself for being happy with you, even for just a little minute. Go away, and leave me to face it out."

"And you'll think it over, Susan, and remember what the doctor says?"

"I can't forget," said she. She meant she could not forget what the doctor had said about the hopelessness of her brother's case; Michael had referred to the plan of sending Willie to an asylum, or madhouse, as they were called in that day and place. The idea had been gathering force in Michael's mind for some time; he had talked it over with his father, and secretly rejoiced over the possession of the farm and land which would then be his in fact, if not in law, by right of his wife. He had always considered the good penny her father could give her in his catalogue of Susan's charms and attractions. But of late he had grown to esteem her as the heiress of Yew Nook. He, too, should have land like his brother--land to possess, to cultivate, to make profit from, to bequeath. For some time he had wondered that Susan had been so much absorbed in Willie's present, that she had never seemed to look forward to his future, state. Michael had long felt the boy to be a trouble; but of late he had absolutely loathed him. His gibbering, his uncouth gestures, his loose, shambling gait, all irritated Michael inexpressibly. He did not come near the Yew Nook for a couple of days. He thought that he would leave her time to become anxious to see him and reconciled to his plan. They were strange lonely days to Susan. They were the first she had spent face to face with the sorrows that had turned her from a girl into a woman; for hitherto Michael had never let twenty- four hours pass by without coming to see her since she had had the fever. Now that he was absent, it seemed as though some cause of irritation was removed from Will, who was much more gentle and tractable than he had been for many weeks. Susan thought that she observed him making efforts at her bidding, and there was something piteous in the way in which he crept up to her, and looked wistfully in her face, as if asking her to restore him the faculties that he felt to be wanting.

"I never will let thee go, lad. Never! There's no knowing where they would take thee to, or what they would do with thee. As it says in the Bible, 'Nought but death shall part thee and me!'"

The country-side was full, in those days, of stories of the brutal treatment offered to the insane; stories that were, in fact, but too well founded, and the truth of one of which only would have been a sufficient reason for the strong prejudice existing against all such places. Each succeeding hour that Susan passed, alone, or with the poor affectionate lad for her sole companion, served to deepen her solemn resolution never to part with him. So, when Michael came, he was annoyed and surprised by the calm way in which she spoke, as if following Dr. Preston's advice was utterly and entirely out of the question. He had expected nothing less than a consent, reluctant it might be, but still a consent; and he was extremely irritated. He could have repressed his anger, but he chose rather to give way to it; thinking that he could thus best work upon Susan's affection, so as to gain his point. But, somehow, he over-reached himself; and now he was astonished in his turn at the passion of indignation that she burst into.

"Thou wilt not bide in the same house with him, say'st thou? There's no need for thy biding, as far as I can tell. There's solemn reason why I should bide with my own flesh and blood and keep to the word I pledged my mother on her death-bed; but, as for thee, there's no tie that I know on to keep thee fro' going to America or Botany Bay this very night, if that were thy inclination. I will have no more of your threats to make me send my bairn away. If thou marry me, thou'lt help me to take charge of Willie. If thou doesn't choose to marry me on those terms--why, I can snap my fingers at thee, never fear. I'm not so far gone in love as that. But I will not have thee, if thou say'st in such a hectoring way that Willie must go out of the house--and the house his own too--before thou't set foot in it. Willie bides here, and I bide with him."

"Thou hast may-be spoken a word too much," said Michael, pale with rage. "If

I am free, as thou say'st, to go to Canada, or Botany Bay, I reckon I'm free to live where I like, and that will not be with a natural who may turn into a madman some day, for aught I know. Choose between him and me, Susy, for I swear to thee, thou shan't have both."

"I have chosen," said Susan, now perfectly composed and still. "Whatever comes of it, I bide with Willie."

"Very well," replied Michael, trying to assume an equal composure of manner. "Then I'll wish you a very good night." He went out of the house door, half-expecting to be called back again; but, instead, he heard a hasty step inside, and a bolt drawn.

"Whew!" said he to himself, "I think I must leave my lady alone for a week or two, and give her time to come to her senses. She'll not find it so easy as she thinks to let me go."

So he went past the kitchen-window in nonchalant style, and was not seen again at Yew Nook for some weeks. How did he pass the time? For the first day or two, he was unusually cross with all things and people that came athwart him. Then wheat-harvest began, and he was busy, and exultant about his heavy crop. Then a man came from a distance to bid for the lease of his farm, which, by his father's advice, had been offered for sale, as he himself was so soon likely to remove to the Yew Nook. He had so little idea that Susan really would remain firm to her determination, that he at once began to haggle with the man who came after his farm, showed him the crop just got in, and managed skilfully enough to make a good bargain for himself. Of course, the bargain had to be sealed at the public- house; and the companions he met with there soon became friends enough to tempt him into Langdale, where again he met with Eleanor Hebthwaite.

How did Susan pass the time? For the first day or so, she was too angry and offended to cry. She went about her household duties in a quick, sharp, jerking, yet absent way; shrinking one moment from Will, overwhelming him with remorseful caresses the next. The third day of Michael's absence, she had the relief of a good fit of crying; and after that, she grew softer and more tender; she felt how harshly she had spoken to him, and remembered how angry she had been. She made excuses for him. "It was no wonder," she said to herself, "that he had been vexed with her; and no wonder he would not give in, when she had never tried to speak gently or to reason with him. She was to blame, and she would tell him so, and tell him once again all that her mother had bade her to be to Willie, and all the horrible stories she had heard about madhouses, and he would be on her side at once."

And so she watched for his coming, intending to apologise as soon as ever she saw him. She hurried over her household work, in order to sit quietly at her sewing, and hear the first distant sound of his well-known step or whistle. But even the sound of her flying needle seemed too loud--perhaps she was losing an exquisite instant of anticipation; so she stopped sewing, and looked longingly out through the geranium leaves, in order that her eye might catch the first stir of the branches in the wood-path by which he generally came. Now and then a bird might spring out of the covert; otherwise the leaves were heavily still in the sultry weather of early autumn. Then she would take up her sewing, and, with a spasm of resolution, she would determine that a certain task should be fulfilled before she would again allow herself the poignant luxury of expectation. Sick at heart was she when the evening closed in, and the chances of that day diminished. Yet she stayed up longer than usual, thinking that if he were coming--if he were only passing along the distant road--the sight of a light in the window might encourage him to make his appearance even at that late hour, while seeing the house all darkened and shut up might quench any such intention.

Very sick and weary at heart, she went to bed; too desolate and despairing to cry, or make any moan. But in the morning hope came afresh. Another day-- another chance! And so it went on for weeks. Peggy understood her young mistress's sorrow full well, and respected it by her silence on the subject. Willie seemed happier now that the irritation of Michael's presence was removed; for the poor idiot had a sort of antipathy to Michael, which was a kind of heart's echo to the repugnance in which the latter held him. Altogether, just at this time, Willie was the happiest of the three.

As Susan went into Coniston, to sell her butter, one Saturday, some inconsiderate person told her that she had seen Michael Hurst the night before. I said inconsiderate, but I might rather have said unobservant; for any one who had spent half-an-hour in Susan Dixon's company might have seen that she disliked having any reference made to the subjects nearest her heart, were they joyous or grievous. Now she went a little paler than usual (and she had never recovered her colour since she had had the fever), and tried to keep silence. But an irrepressible pang forced out the question -

"Where?"

"At Thomas Applethwaite's, in Langdale. They had a kind of harvest-home, and he were there among the young folk, and very thick wi' Nelly Hebthwaite, old Thomas's niece. Thou'lt have to look after him a bit, Susan!"

She neither smiled nor sighed. The neighbour who had been speaking to her was struck with the gray stillness of her face. Susan herself felt how well her self-command was obeyed by every little muscle, and said to herself in her Spartan manner, "I can bear it without either wincing or blenching." She went home early, at a tearing, passionate pace, trampling and breaking through all obstacles of briar or bush. Willie was moping in her absence--hanging listlessly on the farm-yard gate to watch for her. When he saw her, he set up one of his strange, inarticulate cries, of which she was now learning the meaning, and came towards her with his loose, galloping run, head and limbs all shaking and wagging with pleasant excitement. Suddenly she turned from him, and burst into tears. She sat down on a stone by the wayside, not a hundred yards from home, and buried her face in her hands, and gave way to a passion of pent-up sorrow; so terrible and full of agony were her low cries, that the idiot stood by her, aghast and silent. All his joy gone for the time, but not, like her joy, turned into ashes. Some thought struck him. Yes! the sight of her woe made him think, great as the exertion was. He ran, and stumbled, and shambled home, buzzing with his lips all the time. She never missed him. He came back in a trice, bringing with him his cherished paper windmill, bought on that fatal day when Michael had taken him into Kendal to have his doom of perpetual idiocy pronounced. He thrust it into Susan's face, her hands, her lap, regardless of the injury his frail plaything thereby received. He leapt before her to think how he had cured all heart-sorrow, buzzing louder than ever. Susan looked up at him, and that glance of her sad eyes sobered him. He began to whimper, he knew not why: and she now, comforter in her turn, tried to soothe him by twirling his windmill. But it was broken; it made no noise; it would not go round. This seemed to afflict Susan more than him. She tried to make it right, although she saw the task was hopeless; and while she did so, the tears rained down unheeded from her bent head on the paper toy.

"It won't do," said she, at last. "It will never do again." And, somehow, she took the accident and her words as omens of the love that was broken, and that she feared could never be pieced together more. She rose up and took Willie's hand, and the two went slowly into the house.

To her surprise, Michael Hurst sat in the house-place. House-place is a sort of better kitchen, where no cookery is done, but which is reserved for state occasions. Michael had gone in there because he was accompanied by his only sister, a woman older than himself, who was well married beyond Keswick, and who now came for the first time to make acquaintance with Susan. Michael had primed his sister with his wishes regarding Will, and the position in which he stood with Susan; and arriving at Yew Nook in the absence of the latter, he had not scrupled to conduct his sister into the guest-room, as he held Mrs. Gale's worldly position in respect and admiration, and therefore wished her to be favourably impressed with all the signs of property which he was beginning to consider as Susan's greatest charms. He had secretly said to himself, that if Eleanor Hebthwaite and Susan Dixon were equal in point of riches, he would sooner have Eleanor by far. He had begun to consider Susan as a termagant; and when he thought of his intercourse with her, recollections of her somewhat warm and hasty temper came far more readily to his mind than any remembrance of her generous, loving nature.

And now she stood face to face with him; her eyes tear-swollen, her garments dusty, and here and there torn in consequence of her rapid progress through the bushy by-paths. She did not make a favourable impression on the well-clad Mrs. Gale, dressed in her best silk gown, and therefore unusually susceptible to the appearance of another. Nor were Susan's manners gracious or cordial. How could they be, when she remembered what had passed between Michael and herself the last time they met? For her penitence had faded away under the daily disappointment of these last weary weeks.

But she was hospitable in substance. She bade Peggy hurry on the kettle, and busied herself among the tea-cups, thankful that the presence of Mrs. Gale, as a stranger, would prevent the immediate recurrence to the one subject which she felt must be present in Michael's mind as well as in her own. But Mrs. Gale was withheld by no such feelings of delicacy. She had come ready-primed with the case, and had undertaken to bring the girl to reason. There was no time to be lost. It had been prearranged between the brother and sister that he was to stroll out into the farm-yard before his sister introduced the subject; but she was so confident in the success of her arguments, that she must needs have the triumph of a victory as soon as possible; and, accordingly, she brought a hail-storm of good reasons to bear upon Susan. Susan did not reply for a long time; she was so indignant at this intermeddling of a stranger in the deep family sorrow and shame. Mrs. Gale thought she was gaining the day, and urged her arguments more pitilessly. Even Michael winced for Susan, and wondered at her silence. He shrank out of sight, and into the shadow, hoping that his sister might prevail, but annoyed at the hard way in which she kept putting the case.

Suddenly Susan turned round from the occupation she had pretended to be engaged in, and said to him in a low voice, which yet not only vibrated itself, but made its hearers thrill through all their obtuseness:

"Michael Hurst! does your sister speak truth, think you?"

Both women looked at him for his answer; Mrs. Gale without anxiety, for had she not said the very words they had spoken together before? had she not used the very arguments that he himself had suggested? Susan, on the contrary, looked to his answer as settling her doom for life; and in the gloom of her eyes you might have read more despair than hope.

He shuffled his position. He shuffled in his words.

"What is it you ask? My sister has said many things."

"I ask you," said Susan, trying to give a crystal clearness both to her expressions and her pronunciation, "if, knowing as you do how Will is afflicted, you will help me to take that charge of him which I promised my mother on her death-bed that I would do; and which means, that I shall keep him always with me, and do all in my power to make his life happy. If you will do this, I will be your wife; if not, I remain unwed."

"But he may get dangerous; he can be but a trouble; his being here is a pain to you, Susan, not a pleasure."

"I ask you for either yes or no," said she, a little contempt at his evading her question mingling with her tone. He perceived it, and it nettled him.

"And I have told you. I answered your question the last time I was here. I said I would ne'er keep house with an idiot; no more I will. So now you've gotten your answer."

"I have," said Susan. And she sighed deeply.

"Come, now," said Mrs. Gale, encouraged by the sigh; "one would think you don't love Michael, Susan, to be so stubborn in yielding to what I'm sure would be best for the lad."

"Oh! she does not care for me," said Michael. "I don't believe she ever did."

"Don't I? Haven't I?" asked Susan, her eyes blazing out fire. She left the room directly, and sent Peggy in to make the tea; and catching at Will, who was lounging about in the kitchen, she went up-stairs with him and bolted herself in, straining the boy to her heart, and keeping almost breathless, lest any noise she made might cause him to break out into the howls and sounds which she could not bear that those below should hear.

A knock at the door. It was Peggy.

"He wants for to see you, to wish you good-bye."

"I cannot come. Oh, Peggy, send them away."

It was her only cry for sympathy; and the old servant understood it. She sent them away, somehow; not politely, as I have been given to understand.

"Good go with them," said Peggy, as she grimly watched their retreating figures. "We're rid of bad rubbish, anyhow." And she turned into the house, with the intention of making ready some refreshment for Susan, after her hard day at the market, and her harder evening. But in the kitchen, to which she passed through the empty house-place, making a face of contemptuous dislike at the used tea-cups and fragments of a meal yet standing there, she found Susan, with her sleeves tucked up and her working apron on, busied in preparing to make clap-bread, one of the hardest and hottest domestic tasks of a Daleswoman. She looked up, and first met, and then avoided Peggy's eye; it was too full of sympathy. Her own cheeks were flushed, and her own eyes were dry and burning.

"Where's the board, Peggy? We need clap-bread; and, I reckon, I've time to get through with it to-night." Her voice had a sharp, dry tone in it, and her motions a jerking angularity about them.

Peggy said nothing, but fetched her all that she needed. Susan beat her cakes thin with vehement force. As she stooped over them, regardless even of the task in which she seemed so much occupied, she was surprised by a touch on her mouth of something--what she did not see at first. It was a cup of tea, delicately sweetened and cooled, and held to her lips, when exactly ready, by the faithful old woman. Susan held it off a hand's breath, and looked into Peggy's eyes, while her own filled with the strange relief of tears.

"Lass!" said Peggy, solemnly, "thou hast done well. It is not long to bide, and then the end will come."

"But you are very old, Peggy," said Susan, quivering.

"It is but a day sin' I were young," replied Peggy; but she stopped the conversation by again pushing the cup with gentle force to Susan's dry and thirsty lips. When she had drunken she fell again to her labour, Peggy heating the hearth, and doing all that she knew would be required, but never speaking another word. Willie basked close to the fire, enjoying the animal luxury of warmth, for the autumn evenings were beginning to be chilly. It was one o'clock before they thought of going to bed on that memorable night.

Chapter IV

The vehemence with which Susan Dixon threw herself into occupation could not last for ever. Times of languor and remembrance would come--times when she recurred with a passionate yearning to bygone days, the recollection of which was so vivid and delicious, that it seemed as though it were the reality, and the present bleak bareness the dream. She smiled anew at the magical sweetness of some touch or tone which in memory she felt and heard, and drank the delicious cup of poison, although at the very time she knew what the consequences of racking pain would be.

"This time, last year," thought she, "we went nutting together--this very day last year; just such a day as to-day. Purple and gold were the lights on the hills; the leaves were just turning brown; here and there on the sunny slopes the stubble-fields looked tawny; down in a cleft of yon purple slate-rock the beck fell like a silver glancing thread; all just as it is to-day. And he climbed the slender, swaying nut-trees, and bent the branches for me to gather; or made a passage through the hazel copses, from time to time claiming a toll. Who could have thought he loved me so little?--who?--who?"

Or, as the evening closed in, she would allow herself to imagine that she heard his coming step, just that she might recall time feeling of exquisite delight which had passed by without the due and passionate relish at the time. Then she would wonder how she could have had strength, the cruel, self-piercing strength, to say what she had done; to stab himself with that stern resolution, of which the sear would remain till her dying day. It might have been right; but, as she sickened, she wished she had not instinctively chosen the right. How luxurious a life haunted by no stern sense of duty must be! And many led this kind of life; why could not she? O, for one hour again of his sweet company! If he came now, she would agree to whatever he proposed.

It was a fever of the mind. She passed through it, and came out healthy, if weak. She was capable once more of taking pleasure in following an unseen guide through briar and brake. She returned with tenfold affection to her protecting care of Willie. She acknowledged to herself that he was to he her all-in-all in life. She made him her constant companion. For his sake, as the real owner of Yew Nook, and she as his steward and guardian, she began that course of careful saving, and that love of acquisition, which afterwards gained for her the reputation of being miserly. She still thought that he might regain a scanty portion of sense--enough to require some simple pleasures and excitement, which would cost money. And money should not be wanting. Peggy rather assisted her in the formation of her parsimonious habits than otherwise; economy was the order of the district, and a certain degree of respectable avarice the characteristic of her age. Only Willie was never stinted nor hindered of anything that the two women thought could give him pleasure, for want of money.

There was one gratification which Susan felt was needed for the restoration of her mind to its more healthy state, after she had passed through the whirling fever, when duty was as nothing, and anarchy reigned; a gratification that, somehow, was to be her last burst of unreasonableness; of which she knew and recognised pain as the sure consequence. She must see him once more,--herself unseen.

The week before the Christmas of this memorable year, she went out in the dusk of the early winter evening, wrapped close in shawl and cloak. She wore her dark shawl under her cloak, putting it over her head in lieu of a bonnet; for she knew that she might have to wait long in concealment. Then she tramped over the wet fell-path, shut in by misty rain for miles and miles, till she came to the place where he was lodging; a farm-house in Langdale, with a steep, stony lane leading up to it: this lane was entered by a gate out of the main road, and by the gate were a few bushes--thorns; but of them the leaves had fallen, and they offered no concealment: an old wreck of a yew-tree grew among them, however, and underneath that Susan cowered down, shrouding her face, of which the colour might betray her, with a corner of her shawl. Long did she wait; cold and cramped she became, too damp and stiff to change her posture readily. And after all, he might never come! But, she would wait till daylight,if need were; and she pulled out a crust, with which she had providently supplied herself. The rain had ceased,--a dull, still, brooding weather had succeeded; it was a night to hear distant sounds. She heard horses' hoofs striking and splashing in the stones, and in the pools of the road at her back. Two horses; not well-ridden, or evenly guided, as she could tell.

Michael Hurst and a companion drew near: not tipsy, but not sober. They stopped at the gate to bid each other a maudlin farewell. Michael stooped forward to catch the latch with the hook of the stick which he carried; he dropped the stick, and it fell with one end close to Susan,--indeed, with the slightest change of posture she could have opened the gate for him. He swore a great oath, and struck his horse with his closed fist, as if that animal had been to blame; then he dismounted, opened the gate, and fumbled about for his stick. When he had found it (Susan had touched the other end) his first use of it was to flog his horse well, and she had much ado to avoid its kicks and plunges. Then, still swearing, he staggered up the lane, for it was evident he was not sober enough to remount.

By daylight Susan was back and at her daily labours at Yew Nook. When the spring came, Michael Hurst was married to Eleanor Hebthwaite. Others, too, were married, and christenings made their firesides merry and glad; or they travelled, and came back after long years with many wondrous tales. More rarely, perhaps, a Dalesman changed his dwelling. But to all households more change came than to Yew Nook. There the seasons came round with monotonous sameness; or, if they brought mutation, it was of a slow, and decaying, and depressing kind. Old Peggy died. Her silent sympathy, concealed under much roughness, was a loss to Susan Dixon. Susan was not yet thirty when this happened, but she looked a middle-aged, not to say an elderly woman. People affirmed that she had never recovered her complexion since that fever, a dozen years ago, which killed her father, and left Will Dixon an idiot. But besides her gray sallowness, the lines in her face were strong, and deep, and hard. The movements of her eyeballs were slow and heavy; the wrinkles at the corners of her mouth and eyes were planted firm and sure; not an ounce of unnecessary flesh was there on her bones-- every muscle started strong and ready for use. She needed all this bodily strength, to a degree that no human creature, now Peggy was dead, knew of: for Willie had grown up large and strong in body, and, in general, docile enough in mind; but, every now and then, he became first moody, and then violent. These paroxysms lasted but a day or two; and it was Susan's anxious care to keep their very existence hidden and unknown. It is true, that occasional passers-by on that lonely road heard sounds at night of knocking about of furniture, blows, and cries, as of some tearing demon within the solitary farm-house; but these fits of violence usually occurred in the night; and whatever had been their consequence, Susan had tidied and redded up all signs of aught unusual before the morning. For, above all, she dreaded lest some one might find out in what danger and peril she occasionally was, and might assume a right to take away her brother from her care. The one idea of taking charge of him had deepened and deepened with years. It was graven into her mind as the object for which she lived. The sacrifice she had made for this object only made it more precious to her. Besides, she separated the idea of the docile, affectionate, loutish, indolent Will, and kept it distinct from the terror which the demon that occasionally possessed him inspired her with. The one was her flesh and her blood--the child of her dead mother; the other was some fiend who came to torture and convulse the creature she so loved. She believed that she fought her brother's battle in holding down those tearing hands, in binding whenever she could those uplifted restless arms prompt and prone to do mischief. All the time she subdued him with her cunning or her strength, she spoke to him in pitying murmurs, or abused the third person, the fiendish enemy, in no unmeasured tones. Towards morning the paroxysm was exhausted, and he would fall asleep, perhaps only to waken with evil and renewed vigour. But when he was laid down, she would sally out to taste the fresh air, and to work off her wild sorrow in cries and mutterings to herself. The early labourers saw her gestures at a distance, and thought her as crazed as the idiot-brother who made the neighbourhood a haunted place. But did any chance person call at Yew Nook later on in the day, he would find Susan Dixon cold, calm, collected; her manner curt, her wits keen.

Once this fit of violence lasted longer than usual. Susan's strength both of mind and body was nearly worn out; she wrestled in prayer that somehow it might end before she, too, was driven mad; or, worse, might be obliged to give up life's aim, and consign Willie to a madhouse. From that moment of prayer (as she afterwards superstitiously thought) Willie calmed--and then he drooped--and then he sank--and, last of all, he died in reality from physical exhaustion.

But he was so gentle and tender as he lay on his dying bed; such strange, child-like gleams of returning intelligence came over his face, long after the power to make his dull, inarticulate sounds had departed, that Susan was attracted to him by a stronger tie than she had ever felt before. It was something to have even an idiot loving her with dumb, wistful, animal affection; something to have any creature looking at her with such beseeching eyes, imploring protection from the insidious enemy stealing on. And yet she knew that to him death was no enemy, but a true friend, restoring light and health to his poor clouded mind. It was to her that death was an enemy; to her, the survivor, when Willie died; there was no one to love her.

Worse doom still, there was no one left on earth for her to love.

You now know why no wandering tourist could persuade her to receive him as a lodger; why no tired traveller could melt her heart to afford him rest and refreshment; why long habits of seclusion had given her a moroseness of manner, and how care for the interests of another had rendered her keen and miserly.

But there was a third act in the drama of her life.

Chapter V

In spite of Peggy's prophecy that Susan's life should not seem long, it did seem wearisome and endless, as the years slowly uncoiled their monotonous circles. To be sure, she might have made change for herself, but she did not care to do it. It was, indeed, more than "not caring," which merely implies a certain degree of vis inertiae to be subdued before an object can be attained, and that the object itself does not seem to be of sufficient importance to call out the requisite energy. On the contrary, Susan exerted herself to avoid change and variety. She had a morbid dread of new faces, which originated in her desire to keep poor dead Willie's state a profound secret. She had a contempt for new customs; and, indeed, her old ways prospered so well under her active hand and vigilant eye, that it was difficult to know how they could be improved upon. She was regularly present in Coniston market with the best butter and the earliest chickens of the season. Those were the common farm produce that every farmer's wife about had to sell; but Susan, after she had disposed of the more feminine articles, turned to on the man's side. A better judge of a horse or cow there was not in all the country round. Yorkshire itself might have attempted to jockey her, and would have failed. Her corn was sound and clean; her potatoes well preserved to the latest spring. People began to talk of the hoards of money Susan Dixon must have laid up somewhere; and one young ne'er-do-weel of a farmer's son undertook to make love to the woman of forty, who looked fifty-five, if a day. He made up to her by opening a gate on the road-path home, as she was riding on a bare-backed horse, her purchase not an hour ago. She was off before him, refusing his civility; but the remounting was not so easy, and rather than fail she did not choose to attempt it. She walked, and he walked alongside, improving his opportunity, which, as he vainly thought, had been consciously granted to him. As they drew near Yew Nook, he ventured on some expression of a wish to keep company with her. His words were vague and clumsily arranged. Susan turned round and coolly asked him to explain himself, he took courage, as he thought of her reputed wealth, and expressed his wishes this second time pretty plainly. To his surprise, the reply she made was in a series of smart strokes across his shoulders, administered through the medium of a supple hazel-switch.

"Take that!" said she, almost breathless, "to teach thee how thou darest make a fool of an honest woman old enough to be thy mother. If thou com'st a step nearer the house, there's a good horse-pool, and there's two stout fellows who'll like no better fun than ducking thee. Be off wi' thee!"

And she strode into her own premises, never looking round to see whether he obeyed her injunction or not.

Sometimes three or four years would pass over without her hearing Michael Hurst's name mentioned. She used to wonder at such times whether he were dead or alive. She would sit for hours by the dying embers of her fire on a winter's evening, trying to recall the scenes of her youth; trying to bring up living pictures of the faces she had then known--Michael's most especially. She thought it was possible, so long had been the lapse of years, that she might now pass by him in the street unknowing and unknown. His outward form she might not recognize, but himself she should feel in the thrill of her whole being. He could not pass her unawares.

What little she did hear about him, all testified a downward tendency. He drank--not at stated times when there was no other work to be done, but continually, whether it was seed-time or harvest. His children were all ill at the same time; then one died, while the others recovered, but were poor sickly things. No one dared to give Susan any direct intelligence of her former lover; many avoided all mention of his name in her presence; but a few spoke out either in indifference to, or ignorance of, those bygone days. Susan heard every word, every whisper, every sound that related to him. But her eye never changed, nor did a muscle of her face move.

Late one November night she sat over her fire; not a human being besides herself in the house; none but she had ever slept there since Willie's death. The farm-labourers had foddered the cattle and gone home hours before. There were crickets chirping all round the warm hearth-stones; there was the clock ticking with the peculiar beat Susan had known from her childhood, and which then and ever since she had oddly associated within the idea of a mother and child talking together, one loud tick, and quick--a feeble, sharp one following.

The day had been keen, and piercingly cold. The whole lift of heaven seemed a dome of iron. Black and frost-bound was the earth under the cruel east wind. Now the wind had dropped, and as the darkness had gathered in, the weather-wise old labourers prophesied snow. The sounds in the air arose again, as Susan sat still and silent. They were of a different character to what they had been during the prevalence of the east wind. Then they had been shrill and piping; now they were like low distant growling; not unmusical, but strangely threatening. Susan went to the window, and drew aside the little curtain. The whole world was white--the air was blinded with the swift and heavy fall of snow. At present it came down straight, but Susan knew those distant sounds in the hollows and gulleys of the hills portended a driving wind and a more cruel storm. She thought of her sheep; were they all folded? the new-born calf, was it bedded well? Before the drifts were formed too deep for her to pass in and out--and by the morning she judged that they would be six or seven feet deep--she would go out and see after the comfort of her beasts. She took a lantern, and tied a shawl over her head, and went out into the open air. She had tenderly provided for all her animals, and was returning, when, borne on the blast as if some spirit-cry--for it seemed to come rather down from the skies than from any creature standing on earth's level--she heard a voice of agony; she could not distinguish words; it seemed rather as if some bird of prey was being caught in the whirl of the icy wind, and torn and tortured by its violence. Again up high above! Susan put down her lantern, and shouted loud in return; it was an instinct, for if the creature were not human, which she had doubted but a moment before, what good could her responding cry do? And her cry was seized on by the tyrannous wind, and borne farther away in the opposite direction to that from which the call of agony had proceeded. Again she listened; no sound: then again it rang through space; and this time she was sure it was human. She turned into the house, and heaped turf and wood on the fire, which, careless of her own sensations, she had allowed to fade and almost die out. She put a new candle in her lantern; she changed her shawl for a maud, and leaving the door on latch, she sallied out. Just at the moment when her ear first encountered the weird noises of the storm, on issuing forth into the open air, she thought she heard the words, "O God! O help!" They were a guide to her, if words they were, for they came straight from a rock not a quarter of a mile from Yew Nook, but only to be reached, on account of its precipitous character, by a round-about path. Thither she steered, defying wind and snow; guided by here a thorn-tree, there an old, doddered oak, which had not quite lest their identity under the whelming mask of snow. Now and then she stopped to listen; but never a word or sound heard she, till right from where the copse-wood grew thick and tangled at the base of the rock, round which she was winding, she heard a moan. Into the brake--all snow in appearance--almost a plain of snow looked on from the little eminence where she stood--she plunged, breaking down the bush, stumbling, bruising herself, fighting her way; her lantern held between her teeth, and she herself using head as well as hands to butt away a passage, at whatever cost of bodily injury. As she climbed or staggered, owing to the unevenness of the snow-covered ground, where the briars and weeds of years were tangled and matted together, her foot felt something strangely soft and yielding. She lowered her lantern; there lay a man, prone on his face, nearly covered by the fast-falling flakes; he must have fallen from the rock above, as, not knowing of the circuitous path, he had tried to descend its steep, slippery face. Who could tell? it was no time for thinking. Susan lifted him up with her wiry strength; he gave no help--no sign of life; but for all that he might be alive: he was still warm; she tied her maud round him; she fastened the lantern to her apron-string; she held him tight: half-carrying, half-dragging--what did a few bruises signify to him, compared to dear life, to precious life! She got him through the brake, and down the path. There, for an instant, she stopped to take breath; but, as if stung by the Furies, she pushed on again with almost superhuman strength. Clasping him round the waist, and leaning his dead weight against the lintel of the door, she tried to undo the latch; but now, just at this moment, a trembling faintness came over her, and a fearful dread took possession of her--that here, on the very threshold of her home, she might be found dead, and buried under the snow, when the farm-servants came in the morning. This terror stirred her up to one more effort. Then she and her companion were in the warmth of the quiet haven of that kitchen; she laid him on the settle, and sank on the floor by his side. How long she remained in this swoon she could not tell; not very long she judged by the fire, which was still red and sullenly glowing when she came to herself. She lighted the candle, and bent over her late burden to ascertain if indeed he were dead. She stood long gazing. The man lay dead. There could be no doubt about it. His filmy eyes glared at her, unshut. But Susan was not one to be affrighted by the stony aspect of death. It was not that; it was the bitter, woeful recognition of Michael Hurst!

She was convinced he was dead; but after a while she refused to believe in her conviction. She stripped off his wet outer-garments with trembling, hurried hands. She brought a blanket down from her own bed; she made up the fire. She swathed him in fresh, warm wrappings, and laid him on the flags before the fire, sitting herself at his head, and holding it in her lap, while she tenderly wiped his loose, wet hair, curly still, although its colour had changed from nut-brown to iron-gray since she had seen it last. From time to time she bent over the face afresh, sick, and fain to believe that the flicker of the fire-light was some slight convulsive motion. But the dim, staring eyes struck chill to her heart. At last she ceased her delicate, busy cares: but she still held the head softly, as if caressing it. She thought over all the possibilities and chances in the mingled yarn of their lives that might, by so slight a turn, have ended far otherwise. If her mother's cold had been early tended, so that the responsibility as to her brother's weal or woe had not fallen upon her; if the fever had not taken such rough, cruel hold on Will; nay, if Mrs. Gale, that hard, worldly sister, had not accompanied him on his last visit to Yew Nook--his very last before this fatal, stormy might; if she had heard his cry,--cry uttered by these pale, dead lips with such wild, despairing agony, not yet three hours ago!--O! if she had but heard it sooner, he might have been saved before that blind, false step had precipitated him down the rock! In going over this weary chain of unrealized possibilities, Susan learnt the force of Peggy's words. Life was short, looking back upon it. It seemed but yesterday since all the love of her being had been poured out, and run to waste. The intervening years--the long monotonous years that had turned her into an old woman before her time--were but a dream.

The labourers coming in the dawn of the winter's day were surprised to see the fire-light through the low kitchen-window. They knocked, and hearing a moaning answer, they entered, fearing that something had befallen their mistress. For all explanation they got these words

"It is Michael Hurst. He was belated, and fell down the Raven's Crag. Where does Eleanor, his wife, live?"

How Michael Hurst got to Yew Nook no one but Susan ever knew. They thought he had dragged himself there, with some sore internal bruise sapping away his minuted life. They could not have believed the superhuman exertion which had first sought him out, and then dragged him hither. Only Susan knew of that.

She gave him into the charge of her servants, and went out and saddled her horse. Where the wind had drifted the snow on one side, and the road was clear and bare, she rode, and rode fast; where the soft, deceitful heaps were massed up, she dismounted and led her steed, plunging in deep, with fierce energy, the pain at her heart urging her onwards with a sharp, digging spur.

The gray, solemn, winter's noon was more night-like than the depth of summer's night; dim-purple brooded the low skies over the white earth, as Susan rode up to what had been Michael Hurst's abode while living. It was a small farm-house carelessly kept outside, slatternly tended within. The pretty Nelly Hebthwaite was pretty still; her delicate face had never suffered from any long-enduring feeling. If anything, its expression was that of plaintive sorrow; but the soft, light hair had scarcely a tinge of gray; the wood-rose tint of complexion yet remained, if not so brilliant as in youth; the straight nose, the small mouth were untouched by time. Susan felt the contrast even at that moment. She knew that her own skin was weather-beaten, furrowed, brown,--that her teeth were gone, and her hair gray and ragged. And yet she was not two years older than Nelly,--she had not been, in youth, when she took account of these things. Nelly stood wondering at the strange-enough horse-woman, who stopped and panted at the door, holding her horse's bridle, and refusing to enter.

"Where is Michael Hurst?" asked Susan, at last.

"Well, I can't rightly say. He should have been at home last night, but he was off, seeing after a public-house to be let at Ulverstone, for our farm does not answer, and we were thinking--"

"He did not come home last night?" said Susan, cutting short the story, and half-affirming, half-questioning, by way of letting in a ray of the awful light before she let it full in, in its consuming wrath.

"No! he'll be stopping somewhere out Ulverstone ways. I'm sure we've need of him at home, for I've no one but lile Tommy to help me tend the beasts. Things have not gone well with us, and we don't keep a servant now. But you're trembling all over, ma'am. You'd better come in, and take something warm, while your horse rests. That's the stable-door, to your left."

Susan took her horse there; loosened his girths, and rubbed him down with a wisp of straw. Then she hooked about her for hay; but the place was bare of feed, and smelt damp and unused. She went to the house, thankful for the respite, and got some clap-bread, which she mashed up in a pailful of lukewarm water. Every moment was a respite, and yet every moment made her dread the more the task that lay before her. It would be longer than she thought at first. She took the saddle off, and hung about her horse, which seemed, somehow, more like a friend than anything else in the world. She laid her cheek against its neck, and rested there, before returning to the house for the last time.

Eleanor had brought down one of her own gowns, which hung on a chair against the fire, and had made her unknown visitor a cup of hot tea. Susan could hardly bear all these little attentions: they choked her, and yet she was so wet, so weak with fatigue and excitement, that she could neither resist by voice or by action. Two children stood awkwardly about, puzzled at the scene, and even Eleanor began to wish for some explanation of who her strange visitor was.

"You've, maybe, heard him speaking of me? I'm called Susan Dixon."

Nelly coloured, and avoided meeting Susan's eye.

"I've heard other folk speak of you. He never named your name."

This respect of silence came like balm to Susan: balm not felt or heeded at the time it was applied, but very grateful in its effects for all that.

"He is at my house," continued Susan, determined not to stop or quaver in the operation--the pain which must be inflicted.

"At your house? Yew Nook?" questioned Eleanor, surprised. "How came he there?"--half jealously. "Did he take shelter from the coming storm? Tell me,--there is something--tell me, woman!"

"He took no shelter. Would to God he had!"

"O! would to God! would to God!" shrieked out Eleanor, learning all from the woful import of those dreary eyes. Her cries thrilled through the house; the children's piping wailings and passionate cries on "Daddy! Daddy!" pierced into Susan's very marrow. But she remained as still and tearless as the great round face upon the clock.

At last, in a lull of crying, she said,--not exactly questioning, but as if partly to herself -

"You loved him, then?"

"Loved him! he was my husband! He was the father of three bonny bairns that lie dead in Grasmere churchyard. I wish you'd go, Susan Dixon, and let me weep without your watching me! I wish you'd never come near the place."

"Alas! alas! it would not have brought him to life. I would have laid down my own to save his. My life has been so very sad! No one would have cared if I had died. Alas! alas!"

The tone in which she said this was so utterly mournful and despairing that it awed Nelly into quiet for a time. But by-and-by she said, "I would not turn a dog out to do it harm; but the night is clear, and Tommy shall guide you to the Red Cow. But, oh, I want to be alone! If you'll come back to-morrow, I'll be better, and I'll hear all, and thank you for every kindness you have shown him,--and I do believe you've showed him kindness,--though I don't know why."

Susan moved heavily and strangely.

She said something--her words came thick and unintelligible. She had had a paralytic stroke since she had last spoken. She could not go, even if she would. Nor did Eleanor, when she became aware of the state of the case, wish her to leave. She had her laid on her own bed, and weeping silently all the while for her lest husband, she nursed Susan like a sister. She did not know what her guest's worldly position might be; and she might never be repaid. But she sold many a little trifle to purchase such small comforts as Susan needed. Susan, lying still and motionless, learnt much. It was not a severe stroke; it might be the forerunner of others yet to come, but at some distance of time. But for the present she recovered, and regained much of her former health. On her sick-bed she matured her plans. When she returned to Yew Nook, she took Michael Hurst's widow and children with her to live there, and fill up the haunted hearth with living forms that should banish the ghosts.

And so it fell out that the latter days of Susan Dixon's life were better than the former.

Elizabeth Gaskell

Elizabeth Cleghorn Gaskell, née Stevenson (29 September 1810 – 12 November 1865), often referred to simply as Mrs Gaskell, was a English novelist and short story writer during the Victorian era. Her novels offer a detailed portrait of the lives of many strata of society, including the very poor, and are of interest to social historians as well as lovers of literature.[1] Gaskell was also the first to write a biography of Charlotte Bronte, The Life of Charlotte Bronte, which was published in 1857.

Early life

Gaskell was born Elizabeth Cleghorn Stevenson on 29 September 1810 at 93 Cheyne Walk, Chelsea. She was the youngest of eight children; only she and her brother John survived infancy. Her father, William Stevenson, was a Scottish Unitarian minister at Failsworth, Lancashire, but resigned his orders on conscientious grounds and moved to London in 1806 with the intention of going to India after he was appointed private secretary to the Earl of Lauderdale, who was to become Governor General of India. That position did not materialise, however, and instead Stevenson was nominated Keeper of the Treasury Records. His wife, Elizabeth Holland, came from a family from the English Midlands that was connected with other prominent Unitarian families, including the Wedgwoods, the Martineaus, the Turners and the Darwins. After she died 13 months after giving birth to her youngest daughter,[2] she left a bewildered husband who saw no alternative for Elizabeth but to be sent to live with her mother's sister, Hannah Lumb, in Knutsford, Cheshire.[3]

While she was growing up Elizabeth's future was uncertain, as she had no personal wealth and no firm home, though she was a permanent guest at her aunt and grandparents' house. Her father married Catherine Thomson in 1814 and they had a son, William (born 1815), and a daughter, Catherine (born 1816). Although Elizabeth spent several years without seeing her father and his new family, her older brother John often visited her in Knutsford. John was destined for the Royal Navy from an early age, like his grandfathers and uncles, but he had no entry and had to join the Merchant Navy with the East India Company's fleet.[4] John went missing in 1827 during an expedition to India.

Much of Elizabeth's childhood was spent in Cheshire, where she lived with her aunt Hannah Lumb in Knutsford, a town she immortalised as Cranford. They lived in a large red-brick house called Heathwaite, on Heathside (now Gaskell Avenue), which faces the large open area of Knutsford Heath. From 1821 to 1826 she attended a school run by the Miss Byerlys at Barford House, and after that Avonbank in Stratford-on-Avon[2] where she received the traditional education in arts, the classics, decorum and propriety given to young ladies at the time. Her aunts gave her the classics to read, and she was encouraged by her father in her studies and writing. Her brother John sent her modern books, and descriptions of his life at sea and his experiences abroad.[5]

After leaving school at the age of 16, Elizabeth travelled to London to spend time with her Holland cousins.[5] She also spent some time in Newcastle upon Tyne (with the Rev William Turner's family) and in Edinburgh. Her stepmother's brother was the miniature artist, William John Thomson, who in 1832 painted a portrait of Elizabeth Gaskell in Manchester. A bust was sculpted by David Dunbar at the same time.[5]

Married life and writing career

On 30 August 1832 Elizabeth married a Unitarian minister, William Gaskell, in Knutsford. They spent their honeymoon in North Wales, staying with Elizabeth's uncle, Samuel Holland, near Porthmadog. The Gaskells then settled in Manchester, where William was the minister at Cross Street Unitarian Chapel. Manchester's industrial surroundings influenced Elizabeth's writing in the industrial genre. Their first child, a daughter, was stillborn in 1833. A son, William, (1844–45), died in infancy, and this tragedy was the catalyst for Gaskell's first novel, Mary Barton. Their other children were Marianne (1834), Margaret Emily, known as Meta (1837), Florence Elizabeth (1842), and Julia Bradford (1846). Florence married Charles Crompton, a barrister and Liberal politician, in 1863.[2]

In March 1835 Mrs Gaskell began a diary, documenting the development of her daughter Marianne, her views of herself and William as parents, the value she gave to her role as a mother, her religious faith, and, later, the relationship between Marianne and her sister, Meta. In 1836 she co-authored with her husband a cycle of poems, Sketches among the Poor, which was published in Blackwood's Magazine in January 1837. In 1840 William Howitt published Visits to Remarkable Places containing a contribution entitled Clopton Hall by "A Lady", the first work written and published solely by Mrs Gaskell. In April 1840 Howitt published The Rural Life of England, which included her second work, Notes on Cheshire Customs.[2]

In July 1841 the Gaskells travelled to Belgium and Germany, and German literature came to have a strong influence on her short stories. In 1847 she published her first work of fiction, Libbie Marsh's Three Eras, in Howitt's Journal, using the pseudonym "Cotton Mather Mills". Her next work, The Sexton's Hero, was published under the same pseudonym. She made her last use of the pseudonym in 1848, with the publication of her story Christmas Storms and Sunshine. Her first novel, Mary Barton, was published in October 1848.[2]

In 1850 the Gaskells moved to a villa at 84 Plymouth Grove,[6] where Elizabeth wrote her remaining literary works, while her husband held welfare committees and tutored the poor in his study. The Gaskells' social circle included writers, religious dissenters and social reformers such as William and Mary Howitt. Charles Dickens and John Ruskin visited Plymouth Grove, as did the American writers Harriet Beecher Stowe and Charles Eliot Norton, while the conductor Charles Hallé, who lived close by, taught piano to one of their daughters. Her close friend Charlotte Brontë stayed there three times, and on one occasion hid behind the drawing room curtains as she was too shy to meet the Gaskells' other visitors.[7]

In early 1850 Mrs Gaskell wrote to Charles Dickens asking for advice about assisting a girl named Pasley whom she had visited in prison. Pasley provided her with a model for the title character of Ruth in 1853. Lizzie Leigh was published in March and April 1850, in the first numbers of Dickens's journal Household Words, in which many of her works were to be published, including Cranford and North and South, her novella My Lady Ludlow, and short stories.

In June 1855 Patrick Brontë asked Mrs Gaskell to write a biography of his daughter Charlotte, and The Life of Charlotte Brontë was published in 1857. This played a significant role in developing Mrs Gaskell's own literary career.[2] In the biography, Gaskell chose to focus more on Bronte as a woman than as a writer of Romantic fiction.[8]

In 1859 Mrs Gaskell travelled to Whitby to gather material for Sylvia's Lovers, which was published in 1863. Her novella Cousin Phyllis was serialised in The Cornhill Magazine from November 1863 to February 1864. The serialisation of her last novel, Wives and Daughters, began in August 1864 in The Cornhill.[2] She died of a heart attack in 1865, while visiting a house she had purchased in Holybourne, Hampshire. Wives and Daughters was published in book form in early 1866, first in the United States and then, ten days later, in Britain.[2]

The house on Plymouth Grove remained in the Gaskell family until 1913, after which it stood empty and fell into disrepair. The University of Manchester acquired it in 1969 and in 2004 it was acquired by the Manchester Historic Buildings Trust, which then raised money to restore it. Exterior renovations were completed in 2011 and the house is now open to the public.[9][10]

On 25 September 2010 a memorial to Elizabeth Gaskell was dedicated in Poets' Corner in Westminster Abbey. It takes the form of a panel in the Hubbard memorial window, above the tomb of Geoffrey Chaucer. The panel was dedicated by her great-great-great-granddaughter Sarah Prince and a wreath was laid.[11]

Literary style and themes

Mrs Gaskell's first novel, Mary Barton, was published anonymously in 1848. The best-known of her remaining novels are Cranford (1853), North and South (1854), and Wives and Daughters (1865). She became popular for her writing, especially her ghost stories, aided by Charles Dickens, who published her work in his magazine Household Words. Her ghost stories are in the "Gothic" vein, making them quite distinct from her "industrial" fiction.

Even though her writing conforms to Victorian conventions, including the use of the name "Mrs Gaskell", she usually framed her stories as critiques of contemporary attitudes. Her early works focused on factory work in the Midlands. She usually emphasised the role of women, with complex narratives and dynamic female characters.[12]

Themes

Unitarianism urges comprehension and tolerance toward all religions and even though Mrs Gaskell tried to keep her own beliefs hidden, she felt strongly about these values which permeated her works—as in North and South, where "Margaret the Churchwoman, her father the Dissenter, Higgins the Infidel, knelt down together. It did them no harm."[13][14]

Dialect usage

Mrs Gaskell's style is notable for putting local dialect words into the mouths of middle-class characters and the narrator. For example, in North and South Margaret Hale suggests redding up (tidying) the Bouchers' house and even offers jokingly to teach her mother words such as knobstick (strike-breaker).[15] In 1854 she defended her use of dialect to express otherwise inexpressible concepts in a letter to Walter Savage Landor:

... you will remember the country people's use of the word "unked". I can't find any other word to express the exact feeling of strange unusual desolate discomfort, and I sometimes "potter" and "mither" people by using it.[15][16]

She also used the dialect word "nesh" (soft), which goes back to Old English, in Mary Barton:
Sit you down here: the grass is well nigh dry by this time; and you're neither of you nesh folk about taking cold."[17]

and later in 'The Manchester Marriage' [1858]:
Now, I'm not above being nesh for other folks myself. I can stand a good blow,

and never change colour; but, set me in the operating-room in the Infirmary, and I turn as sick as a girl.At Mrs Wilson's death Norah came back to them, as nurse to the newly-born little Edwin; into which post she was not installed without a pretty strong oration on the part of the proud and happy father; who declared that if he found out that Norah ever tried to screen the boy by a falsehood, or to make him nesh either in body or mind, she should go that very day.[18]

Elizabeth Gaskell

Elizabeth Cleghorn Gaskell, née Stevenson (29 September 1810 – 12 November 1865), often referred to simply as Mrs Gaskell, was a English novelist and short story writer during the Victorian era. Her novels offer a detailed portrait of the lives of many strata of society, including the very poor, and are of interest to social historians as well as lovers of literature.[1] Gaskell was also the first to write a biography of Charlotte Bronte, The Life of Charlotte Bronte, which was published in 1857.

Early life

Gaskell was born Elizabeth Cleghorn Stevenson on 29 September 1810 at 93 Cheyne Walk, Chelsea. She was the youngest of eight children; only she and her brother John survived infancy. Her father, William Stevenson, was a Scottish Unitarian minister at Failsworth, Lancashire, but resigned his orders on conscientious grounds and moved to London in 1806 with the intention of going to India after he was appointed private secretary to the Earl of Lauderdale, who was to become Governor General of India. That position did not materialise, however, and instead Stevenson was nominated Keeper of the Treasury Records. His wife, Elizabeth Holland, came from a family from the English Midlands that was connected with other prominent Unitarian families, including the Wedgwoods, the Martineaus, the Turners and the Darwins. After she died 13 months after giving birth to her youngest daughter,[2] she left a bewildered husband who saw no alternative for Elizabeth but to be sent to live with her mother's sister, Hannah Lumb, in Knutsford, Cheshire.[3]

While she was growing up Elizabeth's future was uncertain, as she had no personal wealth and no firm home, though she was a permanent guest at her aunt and grandparents' house. Her father married Catherine Thomson in 1814 and they had a son, William (born 1815), and a daughter, Catherine (born 1816). Although Elizabeth spent several years without seeing her father and his new family, her older brother John often visited her in Knutsford. John was destined for the Royal Navy from an early age, like his grandfathers and uncles, but he had no entry and had to join the Merchant Navy with the East India Company's fleet.[4] John went missing in 1827 during an expedition to India.

Much of Elizabeth's childhood was spent in Cheshire, where she lived with her aunt Hannah Lumb in Knutsford, a town she immortalised as Cranford. They lived in a large red-brick house called Heathwaite, on Heathside (now Gaskell Avenue), which faces the large open area of Knutsford Heath. From 1821 to 1826 she attended a school run by the Miss Byerlys at Barford House, and after that Avonbank in Stratford-on-Avon[2] where she received the traditional education in arts, the classics, decorum and propriety given to young ladies at the time. Her aunts gave her the classics to read, and she was encouraged by her father in her studies and writing. Her brother John sent her modern books, and descriptions of his life at sea and his experiences abroad.[5]

After leaving school at the age of 16, Elizabeth travelled to London to spend time with her Holland cousins.[5] She also spent some time in Newcastle upon Tyne (with the Rev William Turner's family) and in Edinburgh. Her stepmother's brother was the miniature artist, William John Thomson, who in 1832 painted a portrait of Elizabeth Gaskell in Manchester. A bust was sculpted by David Dunbar at the same time.[5]

Married life and writing career

On 30 August 1832 Elizabeth married a Unitarian minister, William Gaskell, in Knutsford. They spent their honeymoon in North Wales, staying with Elizabeth's uncle, Samuel Holland, near Porthmadog. The Gaskells then settled in Manchester, where William was the minister at Cross Street Unitarian Chapel. Manchester's industrial surroundings influenced Elizabeth's writing in the industrial genre. Their first child, a daughter, was stillborn in 1833. A son, William, (1844–45), died in infancy, and this tragedy was the catalyst for Gaskell's first novel, Mary Barton. Their other children were Marianne (1834), Margaret Emily, known as Meta (1837), Florence Elizabeth (1842), and Julia Bradford (1846). Florence married Charles Crompton, a barrister and Liberal politician, in 1863.[2]

In March 1835 Mrs Gaskell began a diary, documenting the development of her daughter Marianne, her views of herself and William as parents, the value she gave to her role as a mother, her religious faith, and, later, the relationship between Marianne and her sister, Meta. In 1836 she co-authored with her husband a cycle of poems, Sketches among the Poor, which was published in Blackwood's Magazine in January 1837. In 1840 William Howitt published Visits to Remarkable Places containing a contribution entitled

Clopton Hall by "A Lady", the first work written and published solely by Mrs Gaskell. In April 1840 Howitt published The Rural Life of England, which included her second work, Notes on Cheshire Customs.[2]

In July 1841 the Gaskells travelled to Belgium and Germany, and German literature came to have a strong influence on her short stories. In 1847 she published her first work of fiction, Libbie Marsh's Three Eras, in Howitt's Journal, using the pseudonym "Cotton Mather Mills". Her next work, The Sexton's Hero, was published under the same pseudonym. She made her last use of the pseudonym in 1848, with the publication of her story Christmas Storms and Sunshine. Her first novel, Mary Barton, was published in October 1848.[2]

In 1850 the Gaskells moved to a villa at 84 Plymouth Grove,[6] where Elizabeth wrote her remaining literary works, while her husband held welfare committees and tutored the poor in his study. The Gaskells' social circle included writers, religious dissenters and social reformers such as William and Mary Howitt. Charles Dickens and John Ruskin visited Plymouth Grove, as did the American writers Harriet Beecher Stowe and Charles Eliot Norton, while the conductor Charles Hallé, who lived close by, taught piano to one of their daughters. Her close friend Charlotte Brontë stayed there three times, and on one occasion hid behind the drawing room curtains as she was too shy to meet the Gaskells' other visitors.[7]

In early 1850 Mrs Gaskell wrote to Charles Dickens asking for advice about assisting a girl named Pasley whom she had visited in prison. Pasley provided her with a model for the title character of Ruth in 1853. Lizzie Leigh was published in March and April 1850, in the first numbers of Dickens's journal Household Words, in which many of her works were to be published, including Cranford and North and South, her novella My Lady Ludlow, and short stories.

In June 1855 Patrick Brontë asked Mrs Gaskell to write a biography of his daughter Charlotte, and The Life of Charlotte Brontë was published in 1857.

This played a significant role in developing Mrs Gaskell's own literary career.[2] In the biography, Gaskell chose to focus more on Bronte as a woman than as a writer of Romantic fiction.[8]

In 1859 Mrs Gaskell travelled to Whitby to gather material for Sylvia's Lovers, which was published in 1863. Her novella Cousin Phyllis was serialised in The Cornhill Magazine from November 1863 to February 1864. The serialisation of her last novel, Wives and Daughters, began in August 1864 in The Cornhill.[2] She died of a heart attack in 1865, while visiting a house she had purchased in Holybourne, Hampshire. Wives and Daughters was published in book form in early 1866, first in the United States and then, ten days later, in Britain.[2]

The house on Plymouth Grove remained in the Gaskell family until 1913, after which it stood empty and fell into disrepair. The University of Manchester acquired it in 1969 and in 2004 it was acquired by the Manchester Historic Buildings Trust, which then raised money to restore it. Exterior renovations were completed in 2011 and the house is now open to the public.[9][10]

On 25 September 2010 a memorial to Elizabeth Gaskell was dedicated in Poets' Corner in Westminster Abbey. It takes the form of a panel in the Hubbard memorial window, above the tomb of Geoffrey Chaucer. The panel was dedicated by her great-great-great-granddaughter Sarah Prince and a wreath was laid.[11]

Literary style and themes

Mrs Gaskell's first novel, Mary Barton, was published anonymously in 1848. The best-known of her remaining novels are Cranford (1853), North and South (1854), and Wives and Daughters (1865). She became popular for her writing, especially her ghost stories, aided by Charles Dickens, who published her work in his magazine Household Words. Her ghost stories are in the "Gothic" vein, making them quite distinct from her "industrial" fiction.

Even though her writing conforms to Victorian conventions, including the use of the name "Mrs Gaskell", she usually framed her stories as critiques of contemporary attitudes. Her early works focused on factory work in the Midlands. She usually emphasised the role of women, with complex narratives and dynamic female characters.[12]

Themes

Unitarianism urges comprehension and tolerance toward all religions and even though Mrs Gaskell tried to keep her own beliefs hidden, she felt strongly about these values which permeated her works—as in North and South, where "Margaret the Churchwoman, her father the Dissenter, Higgins the Infidel, knelt down together. It did them no harm."[13][14]

Dialect usage

Mrs Gaskell's style is notable for putting local dialect words into the mouths of middle-class characters and the narrator. For example, in North and South Margaret Hale suggests redding up (tidying) the Bouchers' house and even offers jokingly to teach her mother words such as knobstick (strike-breaker).[15] In 1854 she defended her use of dialect to express otherwise inexpressible concepts in a letter to Walter Savage Landor:

... you will remember the country people's use of the word "unked". I can't find any other word to express the exact feeling of strange unusual desolate discomfort, and I sometimes "potter" and "mither" people by using it.[15][16]

She also used the dialect word "nesh" (soft), which goes back to Old English, in Mary Barton:
Sit you down here: the grass is well nigh dry by this time; and you're neither of you nesh folk about taking cold."[17]

and later in 'The Manchester Marriage' [1858]:
Now, I'm not above being nesh for other folks myself. I can stand a good blow, and never change colour; but, set me in the operating-room in the Infirmary,

and I turn as sick as a girl.At Mrs Wilson's death Norah came back to them, as nurse to the newly-born little Edwin; into which post she was not installed without a pretty strong oration on the part of the proud and happy father; who declared that if he found out that Norah ever tried to screen the boy by a falsehood, or to make him nesh either in body or mind, she should go that very day.[18]

Printed in Great Britain
by Amazon

31305094R00046